First Published in the United States of America in 2016 by Anthology Editions, LLC

87 Guernsey Street
Brooklyn, NY 11222

anthologyeditions.com
boo-hooray.com

Book produced by Johan Kugelberg/Boo-Hooray for Anthology Editions

Design by Bryan Cipolla

Design Assistant: Christian Mojallali

Edited by Michael P. Daley, Johan Kugelberg, & Gabriel Mckee

Assistant Editor: Mark Iosifescu

First Edition

ARC 028

Printed in China.

ISBN: 978-1-944860-00-4
Library of Congress Control Number: 2016933072

FLYING SAUCERS ARE REAL!

A "saucer crewman" very much like the moon man (or spirit) described by Swedenborg in his writings about the inhabitants of different planets of the solar system with whom, he stated, he had conversations [...] This photograph is from Germany (note trench coats and North European types), but the "saucer crewman" is from a UFO that crashed near Mexico City; the corpses were sent to Germany for study. Was he based on Luna?

— W. Gordon Allen, *Space-Craft From Beyond Three-Dimensions*

FLYING SAUCERS ARE REAL!

THE UFO LIBRARY OF JACK WOMACK

Text by JACK WOMACK • Introduction by WILLIAM GIBSON

Edited by MICHAEL P. DALEY, JOHAN KUGELBERG, & GABRIEL MCKEE

New York City: Anthology Editions, 2016

Thanks to John A. Buchtel, Director of Special Collections at the Lauinger Library, the Jack Womack UFO Library now has a permanent home where it will be preserved and studied at Georgetown University. The work of special collections librarians and archivists like John make it possible for these underexplored narratives to assume their proper place in the history of 20th century popular ideology.

••• CONTENTS •••

Claude Vorilhon ("Raël"). *The Message Given To Me By Extra-Terrestrials: They Took Me To Their Planet.* Tokyo: AOM Corporation, 1986. Mass-market paperback with dust jacket. 295 p. Illustrated. Second English edition; originally published: Montreal: Fondation Pour l'Accueil des Elohim, 1978. Translation of *Le livre qui dit la vérité* and *Les extra-terrestres m'ont emmené sur leur planète.* **Above:** From p. 85.

THE SECRET OF THE SAUCERS

● ● ● ● ● ● ● ● ● ● ● ● ●

Introduction by WILLIAM GIBSON

You hold it now in your hand: the source-code, the veritable root of the enigma. Jack Womack has brought it to the surface for you, via a years-long ritual of great geographical complexity; has assembled, here, out of the world's wrack of lost books, the necessary pentagram of the root-stuff of the saucers. The truth, all these years, hasn't, as *The X-Files* had it, been out there, but rather was in here. Within these peculiar volumes, these testimonials to certain human needs.

My mother saw a saucer in rural Tennessee, shortly after my birth. Or a cigar, rather. A somewhat close encounter, above our rented farmhouse, near Oak Ridge, my father absent on business. She was sole witness. As a child, later, wanting to believe, I "interviewed" her about it. Read books of the sort catalogued here. Pondered. As an adult I began to imagine not the cigar, the row of illuminated windows down each side flashing (her description) as the windows of one passenger train strobe, when viewed from another travelling in the opposite direction, but the farmhouse, its perimeter of electric fence, the dog, the baby (myself), the looming ridge of scrub pine, the darkness unbroken for miles by any streetlight, and her anxiety.

Today I believe that she had been infected, in her loneliness, her anxiety, by what we now think of as a meme.

Jack Womack, over years, assembled this splendid collection of the only physical evidence of the advent of that meme. A library of one very singular flavor of Babel, and now you hold its catalog. His commentary, I believe, admits us to the inner sanctum, the primal moment, the very planet from which the saucers, wingless, nonetheless came winging. He will introduce you to figures from ours, essential linkages, shadowy entities on the far sides of manual typewriters, otherwise lost down the well of time. He will, with acute curatorial instinct and a dry yet gentle humor, reveal their secret.

He has shown me the source of that which my mother saw, of which she told me as a child, and for that, and for this collection, I am very grateful.

Max B. Miller. *Flying Saucers: Fact or Fiction?* Los Angeles: Trend Books, 1957. Pulp magazine-format monograph, perfect bound with staples. 128 p. Illustrated. "Trend Book 145"; "Library edition." **Frank Edwards.** *Flying Saucers–Serious Business.* New York: Lyle Stewart, 1966. Clothbound with dust jacket. 319 p. + [32] p. of plates. Illustrated.

FRANK EDWARDS

flying saucers – serious business

WHAT IS THE TRUTH ABOUT THE STRANGE OBJECTS THAT COME

(continued on front flap)

Max B. Miller, founder of the group Flying Saucers International, organized the first flying saucer convention in the late 1950s. *Flying Saucers: Fact or Fiction?* (1957) was released in advance of the event. Held in Los Angeles at the Hollywood Hotel, the con featured witnesses, writers, and investigators as well as one "Dr. X," who in the great tradition of history's enigmatic figures (Cagliostro, Kaspar Hauser) spoke allusively about saucers, their crews, planets, food, and social lives before returning to his own private aether.

Frank Edwards (1908–1967) employed the skills of a veteran broadcaster in writing *Flying Saucers– Serious Business* (1966), the bestselling popular history of the first twenty years of flying saucer sightings.

FLYING SAUCERS ARE WATCHING YOU

THE INCIDENT AT DEXTER
AND THE INCREDIBLE MICHIGAN FLAP

JOHN C. SHERWOOD

WITH INTRODUCTION BY GRAY BARKER

SAUCERIAN PUBLICATIONS, CLARKSBURG, W. VA.

When John C. Sherwood was seventeen, Gray Barker published his book, *Flying Saucers Are Watching You* (1967), a dry recounting of events during the 1966 Michigan Flap. Barker's congratulation, post-publication: "Evidently the fans swallowed this one with a gulp."

During the UFO Flap of 1965–67, C-List paperback houses (Award, Manor, Tower, Belmont et al.) whipped up slender volumes fitting a standard template to satisfy a non-discerning audience. Steve Tyler's *Are the Invaders Coming?* (1968) is exemplary in both the cut-and-paste qualities of its text and its ad hoc cover art design.

John C. Sherwood. *Flying Saucers Are Watching You: The Incident at Dexter and the Incredible Michigan Flap.* Clarksburg, WV: Saucerian Books, 1967. Perfect bound in wrappers. 78 p. Illustrated. Subtitle from cover. Introduction by Gray Barker. **Steven Tyler.** *Are the Invaders Coming?* New York: Tower Publishing, 1968. Mass-market paperback. 146 p. Illustrated. With an introduction by W.R. Akins.

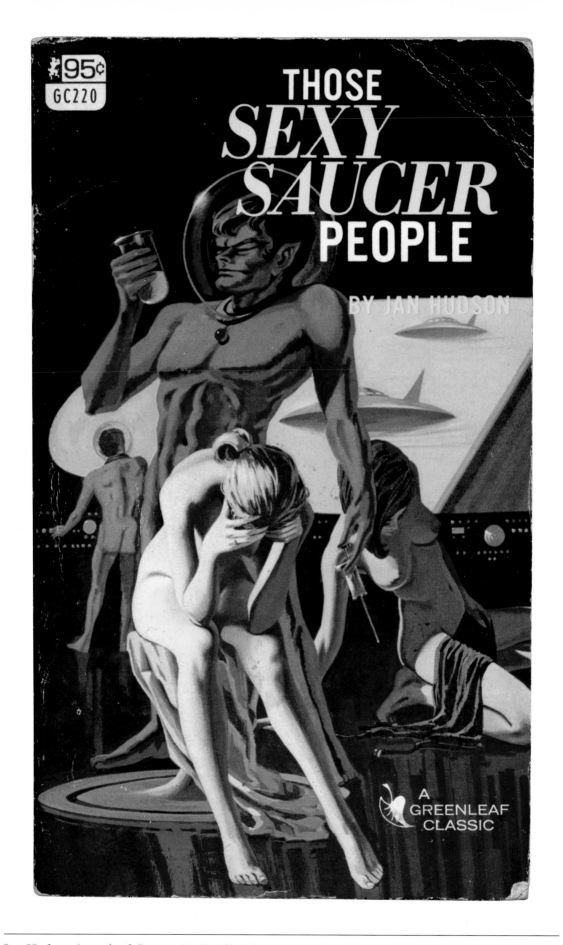

Jan Hudson (pseud. of George H. Smith). *Those Sexy Saucer People.* San Diego, CA: Greenleaf Classics, Inc., 1967. Mass-market paperback. 176 p. **John W. Dean.** *Flying Saucers and the Scriptures.* New York: Vantage Press, 1964. Clothbound with dust jacket. 173 p. + [63] p. of plates. Illustrated.

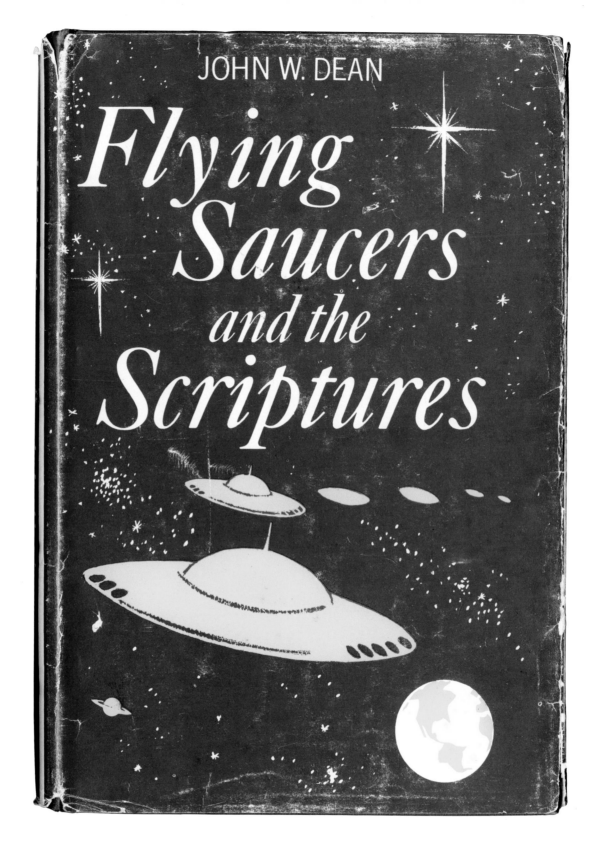

The essence of the Sixties is captured in Ed Smith's cover art for *Those Sexy Saucer People* (1967), written by George H. Smith under the pseudonym Jan Hudson.

Only upon opening *Flying Saucers and the Scriptures* (1964) does it become clear that religion is nearly absent from its pages, and Dean notes he is in fact channeling a Korendian, or human being who lives on the planet Korendar; and presents the Master List Of Planets, along with drawings of space ships, photos of the sky, and pictures of Venusian dogs.

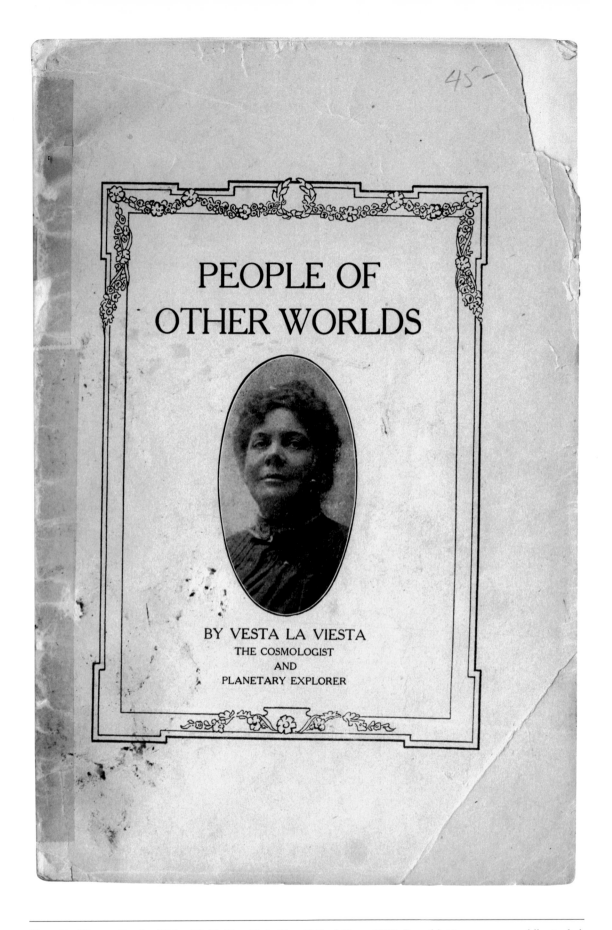

Vesta La Viesta. *People of Other Worlds.* New York: Geo. T. Funk Press, 1923. Pamphlet in wrappers, saddle stapled. 62 p. Betty Hill. *A Common Sense Approach to UFOs.* Greenland, NH: Betty Hill, 1995. Perfect bound in wrappers. 176 p. Illustrated. Inscribed: "[first line obscured by white-out] / Best wishes, / Betty Hill." With many manuscript notes throughout.

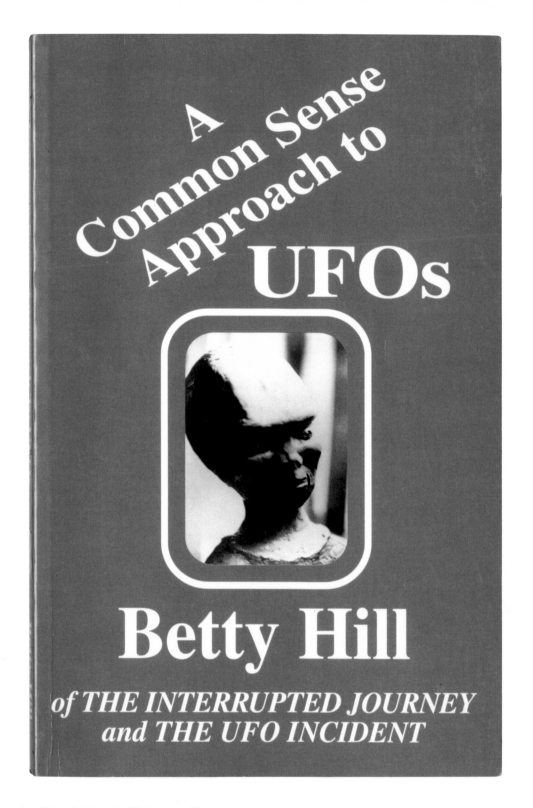

Vesta La Viesta's *People of Other Worlds* (1923) is exemplary channeled wisdom such as that put forth by the roll, like sheet metal, throughout the 19th century, from Moroni's golden plates to endless conversations via mediums with Martians or Jovians.

The best-known saucer "abductees" were Barney and Betty Hill of New Hampshire. In 1965, while under hypnosis, they claimed their car was stopped and that they were taken aboard a spacecraft not to share cosmic wisdom with Space Brothers, but to be questioned and probed by small, humorless gray beings. Betty Hill described her specific experiences–the details of abduction by then familiar in all their contemporary boilerplate–in *A Common Sense Approach to UFOs* (1995).

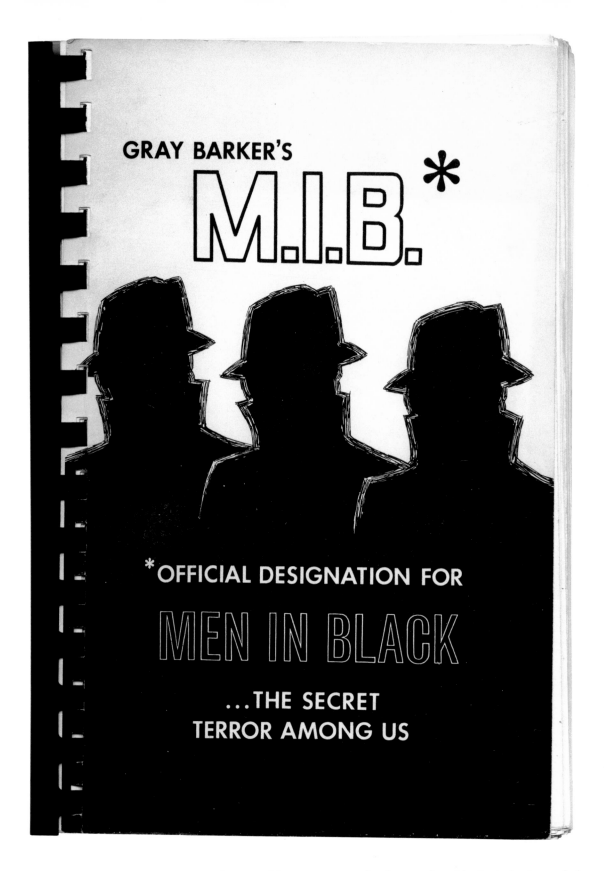

GRAY BARKER'S
M.I.B.*

*OFFICIAL DESIGNATION FOR

MEN IN BLACK

...THE SECRET
TERROR AMONG US

Gray Barker, whose saucer career began with an account of a threatening, black-clad trio, ended with more stories of the same. *M.I.B.: The Secret Terror Among Us* appeared in 1983. In the thirty years since Barker's death, Men in Black have become as American as Ronald McDonald.

In *Round Trip to Hell in a Flying Saucer* (1955), Bakersfield auto mechanic Cecil Michael tells of being taken to the planet Hell, where he meets Satan.

ROUND TRIP TO HELL IN A FLYING SAUCER

By CECIL MICHAEL

Gray Barker. *M.I.B.: The Secret Terror Among Us.* Jane Lew, WV: New Age Press, 1983. In wrappers, comb bound. 159 p. **Cecil Michael.** *Round Trip to Hell in a Flying Saucer.* New York: Vantage Press, 1955. Clothbound with dust jacket. 61 p. + [6] p. of plates. Illustrated.

By the author of
STRANGER THAN SCIENCE
and STRANGEST OF ALL

FRANK EDWARDS

STRANGE WORLD

An ALL NEW collection of *true events*—
118 astounding incidents
so fantastic and amazing as to baffle
the most brilliant scientific mind!

"A FASCINATING BOOK..."
—CHICAGO TRIBUNE

THE FLYING DISCS AS I KNEW THEM

● ● ● ● ● ● ● ● ● ● ● ●

One summer day in 1964 I turned on Lexington's local TV morning show. The hostess dressed in a style one part Derby party, one part Christmas cracker. The host flashed the shins of an albino Rockette each time he crossed his legs. Rather than horses, that morning they raved about a new paperback, Frank Edwards' *Strange World*.

As I write this I am looking at the very copy of *Strange World* my grandmother bought me an hour later, plucked from the black metal paperback rack at Rexall Drugs on East High Street. It is entry number one in the library I went on to build over 40 years, long called "*Human–All Too Human*."

I read the book twice that afternoon, believing the unbelievable. The monster apes of Oregon, the Loch Ness Monster, the Barbados coffins, poltergeists, the man they couldn't hang, plagues of mold, glowing purple blobs in the middle of 26th Street in Philadelphia, and, as per the back blurb, "who–*or what*–painted 'Remember Pearl Harbor' on an Indiana sidewalk two years before the infamous attack?"

And throughout the text, accounts of flying saucers (this was Edwards' last compilation of outré tales, prior to *Flying Saucers–Serious Business*), or rather UFOs, the *au courant* term by the 1960s. To a mid-century child with curious mind yet no interest in science fiction writing even the implications of a purple blob in a street somewhere in Philadelphia stirred thoughts of UFOs, their origins, their pilots, their languages. *If proven*: there were possibilities, there. Flying saucers inspired in me that same sense of wonder about which my friends in science fiction speak. Both were ways to see beyond the neighborhood.

In the literature of the Flying Saucer, Outer Space contains planets, stars, wonders: Venus, Mars, Clarion, Vulcan, crosses on the moon, thunderstones. But, Inner Space? Conspiracy theories, the true meaning of lights in the sky, spiritual messages, government distrust, the escapades of dark-suited men; inferior races, eugenics, the Cosmic Jew, fantasies fascist or murderous; sexual imaginings, confessions of lonely souls, inchoate attempts to understand one's personal visions, spectacularly pointless hoaxes, folk myth, psychological insights, poetry, the perfect lunacy of Holy Fools.

The literature of the Flying Saucer is the literature of the alien most familiar to us.

Frank Edwards. *Strange World.* New York: Ace Books, 1964. Mass-market paperback. 251 p.

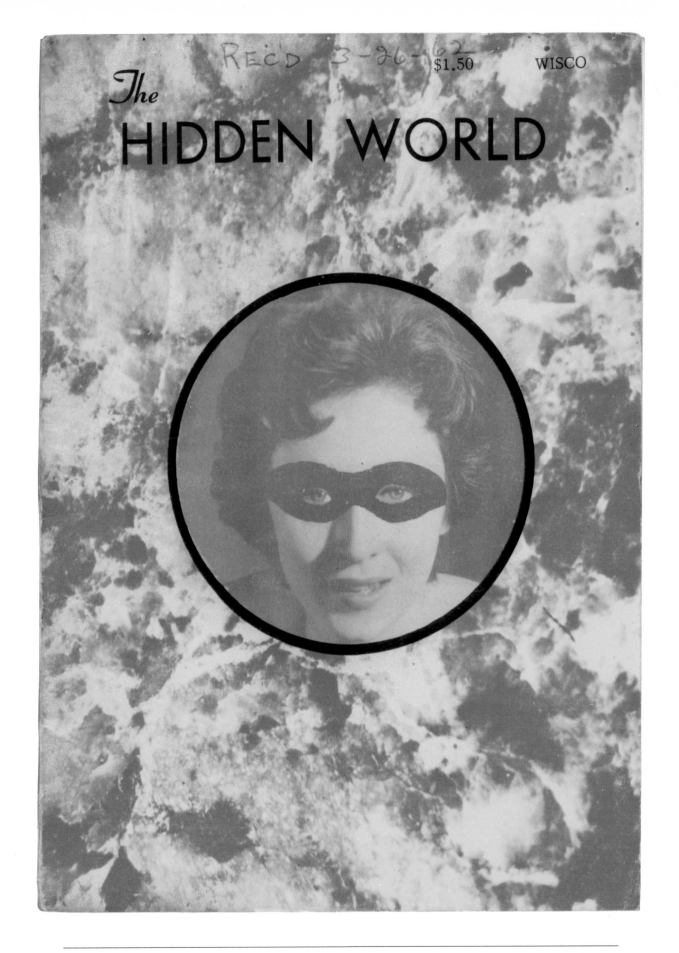

Ray Palmer, ed. *The Hidden World no. B-1 [A-5], Spring 1962.* Mundelein, IL: Palmer Publications, 1962. Pulp magazine in wrappers, perfect bound with staples. pp. 766–956. Illustrated.

ONE MEASURES A CIRCLE, BEGINNING HERE

● ● ● ● ● ● ● ● ● ● ● ● ●

Science fiction black sheep Ray Palmer (1910–1977), First Fandom notable, paterfamilias of much that is postwar popular culture, knew his opportunities when he saw them.

Hired as editor in 1938 to rescue the dying scientifiction pulp *Amazing Stories*, Palmer hired artist Virgil Finlay and bought Isaac Asimov's first published story, "Marooned Off Vesta." Of that first generation of US science fiction editors who made formal the strict parameters and resulting limitations of the genre throughout mid-century, Palmer was notorious even at the time for preferring his space opera slapdash, slam-bang, and science-free.

In 1943 Palmer rescued a letter by Richard Shaver (1907–1975) from the trash. In it Shaver claimed he discovered the alphabet of the world's Ur-language, Mantong. Palmer asked to see more. In return he received 10,000 words entitled "A Warning to Future Man." Shaver's story, in brief: Pre-everything, fifty billion Atlans and Titans, the two original Great Races of Lemuria, lived in beautiful cities throughout the Cavern World, which exists deep within the Earth. When the sun's original protective carbon shell burned away, exposing the Great Ones to dangerous radiation, most of them flew away in rockets, abandoning Earth to the primitive, slow-evolving apes who infested the outer surface. Those Great Ones who for whatever reason stayed behind lost their vitality through constant abuse of stim[ula-tion] machines, eventually degenerating into the Dero, who today use telepathy to lure their victims (female, voluptuous) into caves, or toward the end of the wrong subway platform, or into elevators that lead only to sub-sub basements. Once captured, their victims are tortured, whipped, repeatedly used as sex slaves; their unending screams ceasing only when the Dero finally kill, and eat them.

Only later did Shaver mention to Palmer that he first heard the screams of the tortured through his welding equipment, in Detroit, in 1932.

Palmer rewrote Shaver's fantasies into "fact"-based fiction, retitled the piece "I Remember Lemuria!" and published it in the March 1945 *Amazing* under Shaver's byline. Almost immediately hundreds of letters arrived at the office, some from outraged science fiction fans, but many more from corre-spondents anxious–desperate–to report their own personal experiences with Dero, which Palmer gleefully printed. For two years *Amazing Stories* was all-Shaver all the time; monthly circulation increased by at least 50,000 copies, and *I Remember Lemuria*–a compilation of the early tales–was published in hardcover form by Palmer's new Amherst Press.

What Palmer called the Mystery, fans–notably Forrest J. Ackerman, later editor of *Famous Monsters of Filmland*–called the Hoax. Organizing letter-writing campaigns, they demanded the end of all things Shaverian, furiously certain it gave science fiction a bad name. A born provocateur, Palmer regularly engaged his critics (including the young Harlan Ellison) to irritate them all the more, at

one point raising the possibility that during the war Dero dug underground tunnels leading straight up to concentration camps, for convenience's sake.

Palmer published Shaver-related material in *Amazing* until 1949, at which time he "stepped down" as editor to focus on other projects, notably his non-fiction magazine, *Fate*, and Amherst (which along with Shaver material published books such as *Oahspe*, a Z-list Book of Mormon). Palmer published other magazines including *Mystic* (later, *Search*), and *Other Worlds* (later renamed *Flying Saucers From Other Worlds*; later still, *Flying Saucers*). And, the project which makes one wonder when Palmer began sampling his own supply: sixteen quarterly volumes of *The Hidden World*, hundreds of pages of Shaver material old and new, each issue bearing some of the era's most strikingly surrealistic covers. In 1967 Greenleaf published Palmer's *The Real UFO Invasion*, a paperback reiterating past tales of glory, and an array of blurry photographs. In the 1950s Palmer fell down a flight of stairs in his house; he blamed the Dero.

Shaver settled back into his reclusive life in Arkansas, still seeking physical evidence of the Atlans and Titans. In time he claimed to find such hidden within special rocks–agates he would find, saw into slices and polish, thereafter photographing their interiors and from those photos making paintings of the images of the Great Ones he perceived within the random swirls in the stone. He did this the rest of his life, all the while still participating in *The Hidden World* and other Mystery-focused endeavors. In 1973 Palmer published *The Secret World*, the only collection of Shaver's artwork. His place as a minor American outsider artist presently appears secure.

The
TRUE STORY OF
The SHAVER MYSTERY

Since 1943 the complete realities of the Shaver Mystery have been withheld; now here they are for the world to judge

Ray Palmer, ed. *The Hidden World no. A-1, Spring 1961*. Mundelein, IL: Palmer Publications, 1961. Pulp magazine in wrappers, perfect bound with staples. 192 p. Illustration on opposite page from p. 2729 of: Ray Palmer, ed. *The Hidden World no. A-16, Winter 1964*. Mundelein, IL.: Palmer Publications, 1964. Pulp magazine. Softcover, perfect bound with staples. p. 2685–2876.

Ray Palmer, with Richard Sharpe Shaver. *The Secret World, Volume One, 1975: The Diary of a Lifetime of Questioning the "Facts."* Amherst, WI: Amherst Press, 1975. Pictorial paper-covered boards. 144 p. Illustrated. The first half contains Palmer's autobiographical *Martian Diary*, the second, Shaver's *The Ancient Earth–Its Story In Stone*. Artwork by Shaver, from Palmer and Shaver's *The Secret World*. **Opposite:** Illustrations by Richard Sharpe Shaver, from p. 81, p. 85.

Although this projection painting was not made from the rock slice on the opposite page, it is from a similar slice of a rock book I picked up on my farm in Wisconsin. It is a particularly hard type of stone, and it is packed with images that may be as numerous as the millions of bits of information that can be stored today in crystals by means of laser beams, and extracted in the same way. I often wonder what such a mechanism would reveal to me if I could use it on my rock books. How can I persuade the scientists to try?

— **Richard S. Shaver,** *The Secret World*, p. 85

Richard Sharpe Shaver. *I Remember Lemuria and the Return of Sathanas.* Evanston, IL.: Venture Books, 1948. Clothbound, no jacket (as issued). 215 p.

Kenneth Arnold and Ray Palmer. *The Coming of the Saucers: A Documentary Report on Sky Objects That Have Mystified the World.* Boise, Idaho and Amherst, Wis.: Privately published by the authors, 1952. Clothbound with no jacket (as issued). 192 p. Illustrated. Inscribed by Arnold on front free endpaper: "6/1/52 / To Jimmy / Here it is and / its [sic] positively true / your friend / Ken Arnold."

Kenneth Arnold. *The Flying Saucer As I Saw It.* [N.p.: Privately published], 1950. Pamphlet in wrappers, saddle stapled. [12] p. Illustrated. Signed by Arnold on the front cover.

YOU GOT SHAVER ON MY SAUCER

● ● ● ● ● ● ● ● ● ● ● ●

Even as Ray Palmer prepared to launch a second Shaver-focused pulp (*Other Worlds*) he surely realized the Mystery's popularity was peaking. Then opportunity not merely knocked, but kicked down the door.

On June 24, 1947, commercial pilot Kenneth Arnold (1915–1984) radioed into Yakima, Washington, reporting he saw nine reflective disc-like objects moving 1200 miles an hour in the sky over the Cascades. Once on the ground he retold his story to the editor of the *East Oregonian*, who sent a story out over the Associated Press wire. The words "flying saucers" first appeared in a no-byline Hearst International release dateline June 26. By June 27, Arnold's story had gone worldwide.

Palmer sent a letter to Arnold asking to buy his account of what he saw. Declining payment, Arnold sent in return a copy of his report to the Army Air Corps at Wright Field, Ohio. Palmer reworked the report into a narrative entitled *"I Did See the Flying Discs!"* which he published as the cover article in the first issue of *Fate* magazine the following year.

A few weeks after receiving Arnold's report, Palmer asked him if he'd investigate a sighting of a flying disc in Washington state roughly around the same time he'd seen his saucers. Arnold, in the midst of a debriefing by two Military Intelligence officers in from Washington DC to investigate his own sighting, agreed. Palmer gave him two contact names, Harold Dahl and Fred Crisman.

Leaving the officers behind, Arnold met Dahl in Tacoma, who told him that on June 21, six flying discs ejected shards of lightweight metal over their boat, off Maury Island, in Puget Sound. The metal scared the crew, burned his son, and killed their dog. Back on shore he took his son to the hospital and gave recovered saucer metal–he showed Arnold some pieces as proof–to his boss, Crisman. The next day, said Dahl, a man dressed in a black suit driving a brand new 1947 Buick sedan stopped him and told him they needed to talk. Precisely recounting the events of the day before, he added, "I know more about your experience than you will want to believe," and warned him he'd better not talk to anyone else.

Unexpectedly, when they next met, Dahl said that he and Arnold should continue their interview at his secretary's house, a rundown shack. Once there, Dahl told Arnold that saucers are piloted by man-like beings made visible by A-bomb radiation. Dahl agreed to arrange a meeting with Crisman, who he promised would say more. After leaving that day, Arnold realized that Dahl's secretary was using a piece of "saucer metal" as an ashtray.

The intelligence officers asked if they could attend the meeting with Crisman, delaying their return to DC by one day to do so. On the evening of August 1, Arnold and the officers met with him, who spent hours retelling the same story Dahl told. Around midnight Arnold reminded Crisman that he was supposed to have brought along a box of saucer metal. He explained he'd forgotten it, and needed to go back to his house to see if he could find it. The officers left, infuriated, telling Arnold they'd be flying back to their base immediately.

Next morning, Arnold saw the *Tacoma Times* headline: SABOTAGE HINTED IN CRASH OF ARMY BOMBER AT KELSO. Both officers were on board; both were killed. The reporter said an unidentified source claimed the plane was shot down because it carried "classified material." Arnold, feeling responsible for having gotten the officers involved in the first place, phoned Palmer to say he'd had enough. Only then did Palmer let on that he himself was alerted to the Maury Island incident by Fred Crisman–the same Fred Crisman who in 1946 wrote a letter to *Amazing Stories* recounting wartime battles with Dero, deep in the caves of Burma.

Over the next two days, while he remained in Tacoma (according to his later account in *The Coming of the Saucers*, likely elaborated upon by the editorial hand of Palmer), Arnold was told by Dahl and by other second-hand sources that the two dead officers were in fact alive, but now hidden away by the military; that all examples of saucer metal had been mysteriously substituted with pig iron; that Crisman, feeling the tug of the road, flew off to Alaska; and that the house of Dahl's secretary, once revisited, appeared to have been abandoned for years. When Arnold finally left Tacoma his plane nearly crashed after he stopped to refuel, the fuel switch seeming to turn off automatically as he began his ascent. Recovering, he flew on.

The Maury Island Case, the first UFO incident following Arnold's initial sighting, contains every ingredient for the perfect *X-Files* episode: mysterious lights in the sky, vanishing evidence, peculiar witnesses, scientific details absent of science, strange deaths, unexplained government involvement, cross-purpose conspiracies, puzzled investigators, a story held up as evidence even after its exposure as a hoax. And underlying, all that is Shaverian: tales of hidden societies, underground worlds, lost continents, perfect Masters in all their blonde beauty, dark strangers among us, the slippery gap between chosen realities, animal mutilation, torture, sex, madness, racism, anti-Semitism, and threatening men in black suits driving Buick sedans, which will smell as new in 1967 as they did when first driven off the lot, twenty years earlier.

The Shaver Mystery itself becomes Jesse Garon to the saucers' Elvis Aaron the moment Kenneth Arnold first sees the flying saucers in June 1947.

THIS is the second photograph print of the FLYING SAUCER given to Kenneth Arnold by Military Intelligence of the Fourth Air Force. This shows positive identification of the strange object in reference to the telephone pole and the tree on the left. The actual distance of the object from the ground when the photogrpah was taken, could not be determined, therefore, we have no known distances on which to base its size.

Kenneth Arnold. *The Flying Saucer As I Saw It.* Back cover. **Illustration on p. 32–33:** Kenneth Arnold. "I Did See the Flying Disks!" *Fate,* vol. 1, no. 1 (Spring 1948). Chicago: Clark Publishing Company, 1948.

"I'll never go into the air again without a camera!" declares Kenneth Arnold standing beside his plane the day after observing a train of nine mysterious flying disks.

I DID SEE
THE FLYING DISKS!

by Kenneth Arnold

THE following story of what I observed over the Cascade mountains, as impossible as it may seem, is positively true. I never asked nor wanted any notoriety for just accidentally being in the right spot at the right time to observe what I did. I reported something that I know any pilot would have reported. I don't think that in any way my observation was due to sensitivity of eyesight or judgment other than what is considered normal for any pilot.

On Tuesday, June 24th, 1947, I had finished my work for the Central Air Service at Chehalis, Washington,

4

McCurry Photo

Kenneth Arnold was born March 29, 1915, in Sebeka, Minn. Educated at Minot, N. Dak. Interested in athletics, was all-state end in 1932-33. Football under Bernie Bierman interrupted by knee injury. Employed by Red Comet, Inc., manufacturers of automatic fire-fighting apparatus, in 1938. In 1940 established his own fire control supply company known as the Great Western Fire Control Supply. Handles, distributes, installs fire-fighting equipment in five states. Uses his plane in his work, landing in pastures and mountain meadows. Married, two children.

and at about two o'clock I took off from Chehalis, Washington airport with the intention of going to Yakima, Washington. My trip was delayed for an hour to search for a large Marine transport that supposedly went down near or around the southwest side of Mt. Rainier in the state of Washington. (This airplane has been discovered at the time of this writing—July 29, 1947.)

I flew directly toward Mt. Rainier after reaching an altitude of about 9,500 feet, which is the approximate elevation of the high plateau from which Mt. Rainier rises. I had made one sweep of this high plateau to the westward, searching all of the various ridges for this Marine ship and flew to the west down and near the ridge side of the canyon where Ashford, Washington, is located.

Unable to see anything that looked like the lost ship, I made a 360 degree turn to the right and above the little city of Mineral, starting again toward Mt. Rainier. I climbed back up to an altitude of approximately 9,200 feet.

The air was so smooth that day that it was a real pleasure flying and, as most pilots do when the air is smooth and they are flying at a higher altitude, I trimmed out my airplane in the direction of Yakima, Washington, which was almost directly east of my position, and simply sat in my plane observing the sky and terrain.

5

Although Arnold later said he should never have responded to Palmer's first letter, in 1950 he wrote and with Palmer's help published and distributed a thin, oversize pamphlet entitled *The Flying Saucer As I Saw It*, the text a revision of Palmer's initial revision, with additional illustrations. (Unsigned copies likely do not exist.) In 1952 Arnold agreed to let Palmer co-author *The Coming of the Saucers*, an enlarged edition of the original story along with much additional, if no more enlightening, material on Maury Island. How much of the account is Arnold's and how much Palmer's we can suppose but not know. Arnold continued to do occasional interviews until the 1960s, and ran unsuccessfully for Idaho Lieutenant Governor in 1962.

(As for Fred Crisman, supposed possessor of the saucer metal: Nearly twenty years later, he was subpoenaed by Jim Garrison as part of his investigation of the Kennedy assassination, being evidently the first person Clay Shaw telephoned after the shooting. He never testified. Those who still haunt Dealey Plaza have at times placed him on the grassy knoll, or the railroad viaduct, on the fourth floor of the Texas School Depository, or as one of the three mystery tramps arrested that day by Dallas police. Within the world of the outré, coincidences are inevitably plentiful.)

Ray Palmer. *The Real UFO Invasion.* San Diego, CA: Greenleaf Classics, 1967. Mass-market paperback. 208 p. Illustrated. **Above:** Photograph from p. 176. **Opposite:** Front cover.

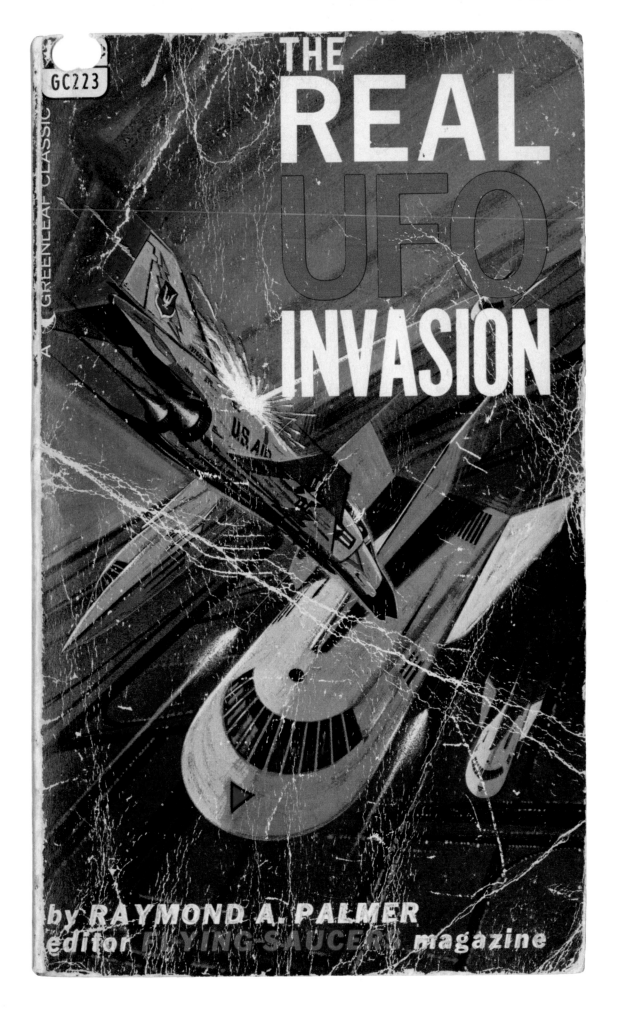

THE REAL UFO INVASION

by RAYMOND A. PALMER
editor FLYING SAUCER magazine

Robert N. Webster, ed. *Fate, vol. 1, no. 1 (Spring 1948)*. Chicago: Clark Publishing Company, 1948. Magazine in wrappers, saddle stapled. 128 p. Illustrated. Contains Kenneth Arnold's "I Did See the Flying Saucers."

$2.50

The COMING of the SAUCERS

By Kenneth Arnold & Ray Palmer

Kenneth Arnold and Ray Palmer. *The Coming of the Saucers: A Documentary Report on Sky Objects That Have Mystified the World.* Boise, ID and Amherst, WI: Privately published by the authors, 1952. Perfect bound in wrappers. 192 p. Illustrated.

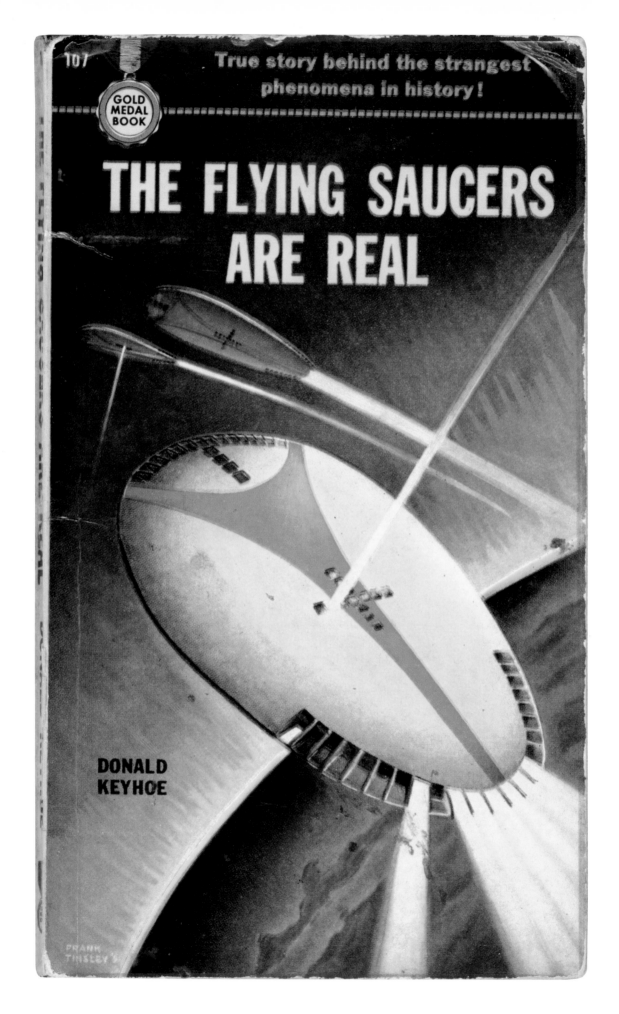

True story behind the strangest
phenomena in history!

GOLD
MEDAL
BOOK

107

THE FLYING SAUCERS
ARE REAL

**DONALD
KEYHOE**

FRANK
TINSLEY

RATIONALISTS & IRRATIONALISTS

● ● ● ● ● ● ● ● ● ● ● ● ●

In 1927 USMC Lt. Donald Keyhoe (1897–1988) accompanied famed pilot Charles Lindbergh on a nationwide flying tour made after Old Lindy's solo crossing of the Atlantic. After writing a bestselling account of the trip, Keyhoe continued writing for both majors (*Reader's Digest*) and pulps (four stories in *Weird Tales*). *The Flying Saucers Are Real* (1950), the first book on flying saucers, bears the finest science fiction cover to ever appear on a non-science fiction book. The text–rich with puzzling lights, conflicting stories, official denials–is the template for all Serious, Thoughtful saucer writing to come. The book sold half a million copies.

Growing suspicious of the government he long served, now-Major Keyhoe retired, picking up the saucer story as he saw it in his next book, *Flying Saucers From Outer Space* (1953), before going the full Mulder in *The Flying Saucer Conspiracy* (1956). In mid-decade he co-founded the National Investigations Committee on Aerial Phenomena (NICAP), whose goal was to make Congress hold hearings examining saucer evidence–to what ultimate purpose was never quite clear. His *Flying Saucers: Top Secret* (1960), continuing in the same vein though with a certain sense of resignation becoming less ignorable in the text, rounded out the decade. NICAP's website (last updated 1997) calls Keyhoe their "spiritual leader."

The second published book on flying saucers took the opposite approach from Keyhoe's, inviting greater leeway for imagination. In his *Variety* column in 1949, reporter Frank Scully (1892–1964) broke the story of alien bodies recovered from a crashed saucer in the western desert and hidden by the military, the first time such a claim was publicly made. Expanding upon his scoop in *Behind the Flying Saucers* (1950), Scully revealed that in fact four magnetically propelled discs 100 feet in diameter had crashed in New Mexico and Arizona. Two years later, it came out that Scully's sources were longtime frauds, and specialists in oil dowsing. The one who posed as a scientist named "Dr. Gee" was said by Scully to have "more degrees than a thermometer." The book nevertheless sold 60,000 copies, far more than his preceding work, *Fun In Bed*.

The character in *The X-Files* named Dana Scully is an admitted homage.

Donald E. Keyhoe. *The Flying Saucers Are Real.* New York: Fawcett Publications, 1950. Mass-market paperback. 175 p. "Gold Medal Book."

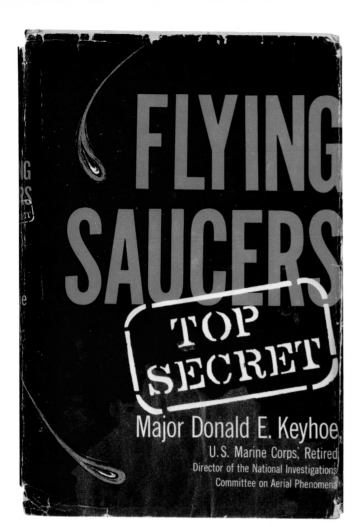

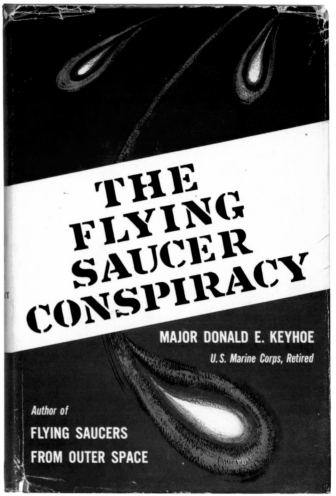

Donald E. Keyhoe. *Flying Saucers: Top Secret.* New York: G.P. Putnam's Sons, 1960. Imitation leatherbound with dust jacket. 283 p. Previous owner's signature on front free endpaper. **Donald E. Keyhoe.** *The Flying Saucer Conspiracy.* New York: Fieldcrest Publishing Co., Inc., 1955. Clothbound with dust jacket. 315 p. **Donald E. Keyhoe.** *Flying Saucers from Outer Space.* New York: Henry Holt and Company, 1953. Clothbound with dust jacket. 276 p. Illustrated.

FLYING SAUCERS

from

outer space

Major DONALD E. KEYHOE
U. S. MARINE CORPS (ret.)

IMPORTANT: SEE BACK OF JACKET

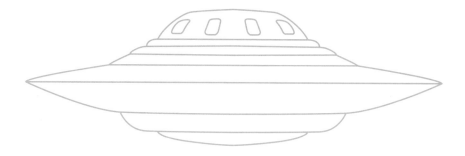

"Finally, we decided that it was probably safe," the doctor said, "as nothing had transpired inside the ship to indicate that there was life therein. Apparently there was no door to what unquestionably was the cabin. The outside surface showed no marking of any sort, except for a broken porthole, which appeared on first examination to be of glass. On closer examination we found it was a good deal different from any glass in this country. Finally, we took a large pole and rammed a hole through this defect in the ship.

"Having done this, we looked into the interior. There we were able to count sixteen bodies, that ranged in height from about 36 to 42 inches. [...] We took the little bodies out, and laid them on the ground. We examined them and their clothing. I remember one of our team saying, 'That looks like the style of 1890.' We examined the bodies very closely and carefully. They were normal from every standpoint and had no appearance of being what we call on this planet 'midgets.' They were small in stature but well proportioned. The only trouble was that their skin seemed to be charred a very dark chocolate color. About the only thing that we could decide at the time was that the charring had occurred somewhere in space and that their bodies had been burned as a result of air rushing through that broken porthole window, or something going wrong with the means by which the ship was propelled and the cabin pressured."

— Frank Scully, *Behind the Flying Saucers*, pp. 128–129

Frank Scully. *Behind the Flying Saucers.* New York: Henry Holt and Company, 1950. Clothbound with dust jacket. xvi, 230 p. **Opposite:** Illustration from Wendelle C. Stevens and August C. Roberts. *UFO Photographs Around the World.* Tucson, Ariz. UFO Photo Archives, 1985–1986. Volume 1, p. 104.

THE RIDDLE OF THE
FLYING SAUCERS
is another World watching?

GERALD HEARD

Photograph taken by Enrique Hausemann Muller, a news-reel cameraman in the Balearie Islands.

After giving long thought to the nature of alien consciousness, Gerald Heard (1889–1971), philosopher and friend of Aldous Huxley and Christopher Isherwood, suggested in his *The Riddle of the Flying Saucers: Is Another World Watching?* (1950) that the pilots of the saucers would prove to be vastly intelligent insects.

> A Martian of any kind, of human, mammal or indeed of any build but that of an insect, would be in much the situation on this Earth as we would be in on Jupiter. But, if he or it were an insect, he or it would have the intense strength which insects show here. Their flight alone, their wing power, is the release of an energy which an elephant might envy. Their four-wing 'vortex flight' is real flight, not the clumsy skidding and flapping on the air which is all the birds can do, and which we somewhat more clumsily imitate. Indeed their wonderful natural flight may have been what first turned the rulers of the Martian insect world to think of artificial flight, as we know the flight of birds gave man the inspiration to follow them into the air.

— Gerald Heard, *The Riddle of the Flying Saucers*, p. 122

Gerald Heard. *The Riddle of the Flying Saucers: Is Another World Watching?* London: Carroll & Nicholson, 1950. Clothbound with dust jacket. 157 p. + [4] p. of plates. **Above:** Photo from plate opposite p. 65.

H.T. Wilkins (1883-1960) was a multilingual Cambridge graduate who worked as a journalist. His first book, *Great English Schools*, appeared in 1925. During the thirties he published several volumes on treasure hunting and pirates, all quite entertaining if you're in the right mood. As was said of the mystery writer Harry Stephen Keeler, Mr. Wilkins' books, to the inexperienced, read as if they might have been written in Choctaw. His stylistic idiosyncracies are evident throughout his work—his fondness for exclamation points, his periodic apostrophes to Mankind at Large, his fear of understatement, his tendency to allow the narrative to drift into unrelated tangents (and tangents within tangents) for pages at a time, his desire never to say "cat" when "carnivorous assailant of the domestic rodential kingdom" will do, his propensity to scatter inscrutable foreign words and phrases throughout his text *sans* translation.

And, most delightfully, his breathtaking willingness to believe anything. We have an inkling that Wilkins would have jumped at the chance to sell his house, his firstborn, or his soul for a seventh-hand account of a lake monster sighting, a treasure map scrawled in crayon on a sheet of typing paper, or a bag of magic beans.

Long interested in Forteana and mysterious phenomena, late in life he turned his attention to flying saucers. *Flying Saucers On the Moon* (published as *Flying Saucers On the Attack* in the US, 1955) showcases his inimitable style, applied to the subject. The lights seen in the sky are, at various times, "gleaming silvery viamanas," "vast, bat-like machines," and "colossal death ray aeroforms." Describing himself as "an open-minded skeptic" he proceeds to tell of an alien spotted in a small restaurant in Kentucky recognizable as such by his "*five-toed shoes*" [ital. in original]. Wilkins is certainly one of the most enjoyable (and unreliable) of enjoyably unreliable narrators. His following work, *Flying Saucers Uncensored* (1956) is even more delirious. Wilkins is known to have finished the manuscript for a third saucer book, *The Phantom War of the Flying Saucers*, before his death, but its present location is tragically unclear.

No one knows why some of the discs are noiseless, and why others emit distinct sounds. Nor do we understand how some of them can attain the fantastic speed of 5 miles a second, as the Washington (D.C.) airport radar and the theodolite calculated, when the saucers were seen for a long time over that airport, and even cruising high over the White House, in 1952! That riddle seems to be connected rather with a fourth dimensional plane of existence than with phenomena of our own normal third-dimensional world.

— **Harold T. Wilkins,** *Flying Saucers on the Moon*, **p. 291**

Harold T. Wilkins. *Flying Saucers on the Moon.* London: Peter Owen Limited, 1954. Clothbound with dust jacket. 329 p. + [8] leaves of plates. Illustrated. Published in the US as *Flying Saucers on the Attack.*

Flying
Saucers
on the Moon

By
H. T. Wilkins

Harold T. Wilkins. *Flying Saucers on the Attack*. New York: The Citadel Press, 1954. Clothbound with dust jacket, 329 p. + [8] leaves of plates. Illustrated.

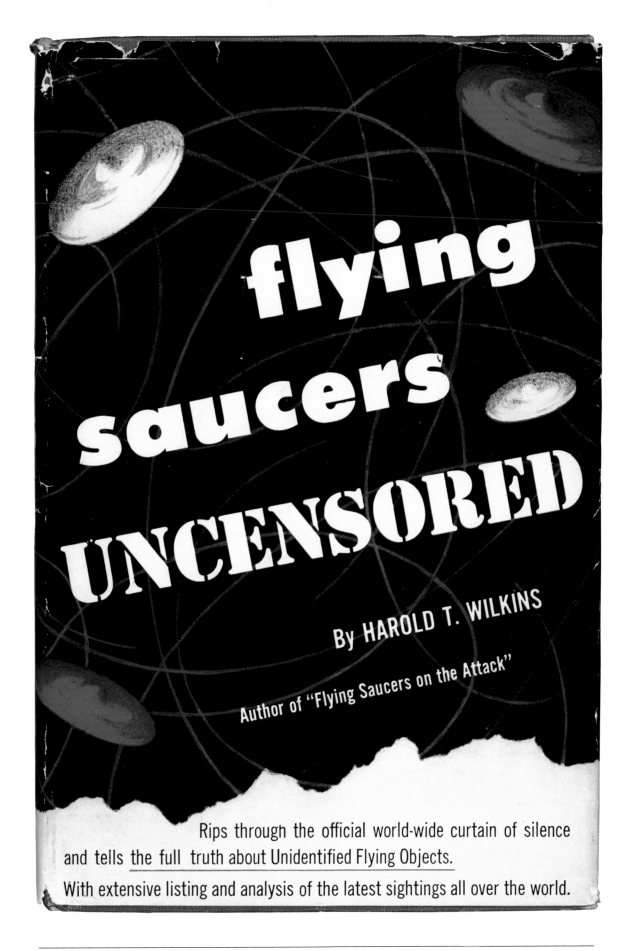

flying
saucers
UNCENSORED

By HAROLD T. WILKINS

Author of "Flying Saucers on the Attack"

Rips through the official world-wide curtain of silence and tells the full truth about Unidentified Flying Objects.

With extensive listing and analysis of the latest sightings all over the world.

Harold T. Wilkins. *Flying Saucers Uncensored.* New York: The Citadel Press, 1955. Clothbound with dust jacket, 255 p. Illustrated.

Other UK writers approached the matter of Flying Saucers with calm, reason, scientific knowledge, and an absence of piffle. Waveney Girvan's *Flying Saucers and Common Sense* (1956) is a fine example of considering our Vauxhall Wyverns of fire. With others, Girvan began publishing *The Flying Saucer Review* in 1955, which remains the field's most respectable publication. Three years later the magazine's first and only annual comp of sightings appeared, *The Flying Saucer Review's World Roundup* (1958).

Left: A Flying Saucer, taken by Juan Coll and Jose Antonio Baena near Malaga on 2nd November, 1954, reproduced in the Spanish evening paper *Madrid*. **Right:** An unusually clear photograph of a saucer over San Francisco.

Waveney Girvan. *Flying Saucers and Common Sense.* New York: The Citadel Press, 1956. Clothbound with dust jacket. 157 p. Illustrated. 1st American edition, February 1956 (c. 1955). **Left:** Photo from plate opposite p. 97. **Flying Saucer Review.** *The Flying Saucer Review's World Roundup of UFO Sightings and Events.* New York: The Citadel Press, 1958. Clothbound with dust jacket. 224 p. + [4] p. of plates. Illustrated. **Right:** Photo from p. 97.

I will now chance my arm at prophecy. I believe that from now on landing reports will become more and more frequent. The researcher after the truth must therefore be very much on his guard not only against the hoaxer, but almost as much against the mocker and the conventionaliser. Earlier in this book I have devoted much space to the conventionalisations which have been used to explain away the flying saucer. Actual landings will be more difficult to deal with, for more positive evidence is offered, or may be offered. For instance, even Dr. Menzel will not be able to say that what actually happened was that two men wearing diving helmets walked out of a temperature inversion. The Astronomer Royal, energetic though he has proved himself in the past, will hardly be brazen enough to suggest that a mock sun has brought us a couple of visitors, though I do believe that Mr. Chapman Pincher would be equal to the task.

— **Waveney Girvan, *Flying Saucers and Common Sense*, p. 131**

Flying Saucer Review. *The Flying Saucer Review's World Roundup of UFO Sightings and Events.* New York: The Citadel Press, 1958. Clothbound with dust jacket. 224 p. + [4] p. of plates. Illustrated. **Waveney Girvan.** *Flying Saucers and Common Sense.* New York: The Citadel Press, 1956. Clothbound with dust jacket. 157 p. Illustrated. 1st American edition, February 1956 (c. 1955).

flying saucers

and
common sense

WAVENEY GIRVAN

the complete answer to the skeptic's case
by an outstanding authority

Aimé Michel (1919–1992) published the first book on flying saucers in French, a straightforward account entitled *Lueurs sur les soucoupes volantes* (published in English as *The Truth About Flying Saucers*, 1956). With the assistance of Jacques Bergier he developed "orthotenics," which proposes that saucer sightings cluster along a rational series of straight lines that overlay the world. (With Louis Pauwels, Bergier later wrote the 60s subcultural, hallucinogenic classic *The Morning of the Magicians*, featuring long-secret societies, stories of Nazi runes, tales of the bodies of gloved Tibetan monks found in the burning ruins of wartime Berlin.)

In Michel's second book, *Mystérieux objets célestes* (*Flying Saucers and the Straight Line Mystery*, 1958), he discusses a wave of French sightings that to his mind more or less prove the geomantic evidence. Most of Michel's works have not been translated into English.

The sensible course, in my opinion is to recognize that unexplained phenomena have been observed in the sky by thousands of people, or perhaps, by now, by tens of thousands.

These phenomena, which have hitherto resisted all attempts at explanation, all present the same strange but definite characteristics, and it is those characteristics which constitute the inexplicable element. They are what Captain Clérouin and Lieutenant Plantier have called *the four mysteries of the saucers*: the mystery of their tremendous and repeated accelerations, apparently conflicting with the mechanical law of mass-ratios; the mystery of their resistance to the vast amount of heat which the friction of the machine against the surrounding air should generate; the mystery of their silence—no whistling sound, no supersonic boom; lastly, the mystery of their changes of shape.

— **Aimé Michel, *The Truth About Flying Saucers*, p. 192**

Bullets whistle, shells whine, jet planes make an infernal din. When they "break the sound barrier" there is an explosion violent enough to break windows and bring down walls. All this is normal. [...] Yet saucers make no noise whatever. Apart from very rare exceptions (the Bouffioulx case is a noteworthy example), the saucers are absolutely silent. Here again, science and observation cannot be reconciled.

— **Aimé Michel, *The Truth About Flying Saucers*, p. 195**

Aimé Michel. *The Truth About Flying Saucers.* New York: Criterion Books, 1956. Clothbound with dust jacket. 255 p. + [14] p. of plates. Illustrated. Translated from the French by Paul Selver.

THE TRUTH ABOUT
FLYING
SAUCERS

Aimé
Michel

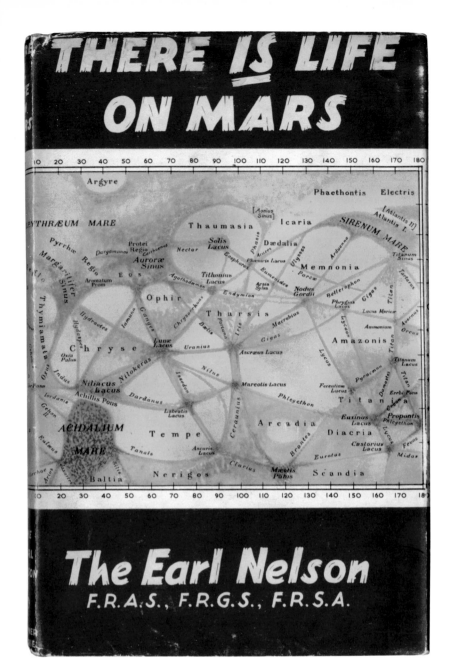

In *There Is Life On Mars* (1955) the Earl Nelson presents theories flawless save for their total reliance upon the existence of Martian canals.

Leonard Stringfield (opposite page) founded CRIFO (Civilian Research, Interplanetary Flying Objects) to serve as a "civilian clearing house" for saucer information featured in his southern Ohio regional newsletter *Orbit*. In the foreword of his *Inside Saucer Post …3-0 Blue* (1957) he explains: *"In these few words is revealed the silent 'other side' of CRIFO's operations, which had its beginning in September 1955 when the Air Defense Command Filter Center in Columbus, Ohio, officially designated my home as a 'UFO reporting post.' For this duty, my home telephone was cleared and I was assigned a code name, which was in part '…3-0 Blue.'"* (p. 5) The text recounts saucer sightings, seeming military and press conspiracies, odd rumors, most though not all taking place in or around Cincinnati.

The Earl Nelson [Earl Albert Francis Joseph Horatio Nelson]. *There IS Life on Mars.* London: Werner Laurie, 1955. Clothbound with dust jacket. 142 p. + [4] p. of plates. Illustrated. **Leonard H. Stringfield.** *Inside Saucer Post …3-0 Blue: CRIFO Views the Status Quo: A Summary Report.* Cincinnati: Civilian Research, Interplanetary Flying Objects (CRIFO), 1957. Perfect bound in wrappers. 94 p. Illustrated. Signed by the author on the title page.

inside

SAUCER POST ...3-0 BLUE

CRIFO views the status quo:

a summary report by

Leonard H. Stringfield

Carl G. Jung (1875–1961), founder of analytical psychology, was long interested in religious aspects of the human psyche, investigating such matters as dream analysis, coincidence, alchemy, astrology, and other borderline subjects. In *Flying Saucers: A Modern Myth of Things Seen in the Sky* (1959) he supposes both saucers and their aliens to be hallucinations, projections of religious longing that have emerged in the anxieties of the postwar era via humanity's collective unconscious. Longtime investigators in the field chuckled at the impossibility of such a theory, and returned to examinations of contrails, space amoebas, and the like.

The apparent increase in Ufo sightings in recent years has caused disquiet in the popular mind and might easily give rise to the conclusion that, if so many spaceships appear from the beyond, a corresponding number of deaths might be expected. We know that such phenomena were interpreted like this in earlier centuries: they were portents of a "great dying", of war and pestilence, like the dark premonitions that underlie our modern fear. One ought not to assume that the great masses are so enlightened that hypotheses of this kind can no longer take root.

— C.G. Jung, *Flying Saucers*, pp. 82–83

So far as I know it remains an established fact, supported by numerous observations, that Ufos have not only been seen visually but have also been picked up on the radar screen and have left traces on the photographic plate. I base myself here not only on the comprehensive reports by Ruppelt and Keyhoe, which leave no room for doubt in this regard, but also on the fact that the astrophysicist, Professor Menzel, has not succeeded, despite all his efforts, in offering a satisfying scientific explanation of even one authentic Ufo report. It boils down to nothing less than this: that either psychic projections throw back a radar echo, or else the appearance of real objects affords an opportunity for mythological projections.

— C.G. Jung, *Flying Saucers*, pp. 146–147

C.G. Jung. *Flying Saucers: A Modern Myth of Things Seen in the Skies.* New York: Harcourt, Brace and Company, 1959. Clothbound with dust jacket. xiv, 186 p. Illustrated. Translated from the German by R.F.C. Hull. First American edition.

Ivan T. Sanderson (1911–1973), graduate of Eton and Cambridge, jungle naturalist and popular writer since the 1930s, was in charge of counter-espionage in the Caribbean for British Naval Intelligence during the war, and was for three decades seen regularly on TV as an animal expert. Long interested in the paranormal, employing logical arguments but prone to beginning from untenable theses, he turned his attention to UFOs in *Uninvited Visitors* (1967), one of the high points of the literature. The cover's 3-D lenticular drew more attention than the contents, which include, along with much else that is iffy, the first nationwide publication of the Allende letters in book form.

If the thing—the first one, that is—*was* a crashed and crippled space creature and still "alive," and the government got wind of it, no wonder there was a sort of jazz-hop among the higher levels to "get that thing out of there" or, alternatively, to dig up a red herring like some good dead whale—pronto. The latter seems to have come to hand—most conveniently and not too far away at that—so the whole area was immediately closed to newsmen and other prying eyes, especially with cigarette lighters! Incidentally, bits of rotten whales are a common feature all around Tasmania as a result of the circum-Antarctic oceanic currents that wash up bits and pieces from the international whaling industry farther south, and especially after really bad storms. In fact, if there had not been any already there, some could quite well have been obtained in short order and dumped there to be examined at leisure by an official party.

Altogether, as a biologist, I am left with a most unpleasant feeling about this whole case. The story as printed in the local press, and the official correspondence and documents I have been able to receive or have seen, just does not conform to reality, and the whole situation seems terribly strange. If it was just another phony sea-monster, then let's have done with it—though I would wish that all governments would always take as much pains with such items, as thereby we might gain some rather interesting new zoological specimens. If it was something else, either let us hear about it, or be told simply that it "is not in the interest of national security"—then we'll drop it.

— **Ivan T. Sanderson,** *Uninvited Visitors,* **pp. 107–108**

Ivan T. Sanderson. *Uninvited Visitors: A Biologist Looks at UFO's.* New York: Cowles Education Corporation, 1967. Clothbound with die-cut dust jacket and lenticular print on front board. viii, 244 p. Illustrated. Image from front board.

T.M. Wright's *Intelligent Man's Guide to Flying Saucers* was published in 1968 as a corrective to the hundreds of titles on the shelves whose authors he perceived as being wildly gullible when it came to saucer tales, but gullibility continued to win the day.

T.M. Wright. *The Intelligent Man's Guide to Flying Saucers.* South Brunswick, NJ/London: A.S. Barnes and Company/ Thomas Yoseloff Ltd., 1968. Clothbound with dust jacket. 279 p. + [28] p. of plates. Illustrated. **Opposite:** Photos from plate [5].

15 November 1978, 16:00, Ipamari, Goyas, Brazil. Sr. Roberto Edilson Perez snapped 4 clear photos of UFO over his estancia.

UFO Photographs Around the World Vols. 1 and 2, by Wendelle Stevens & August C. Roberts offers the most complete compilation of lens flares, camera smudges, film imperfections, blurs, and jiggled shots ever published.

Opposite: *First of a series of photos taken by George J. Stock of Trenton, New Jersey, on July 29, 1952.* From T. M. Wright, *The Intelligent Man's Guide to Flying Saucers,* plate [14]. **Wendelle C. Stevens and August C. Roberts.** *UFO Photographs Around the World.* Tucson, AZ: UFO Photo Archives, 1985–1986. Imitation leatherbound with dust jacket. 2 vols. (256, 256 p.). Illustrated. Vol. 2 is dated 1985, vol. 1 is 1986.

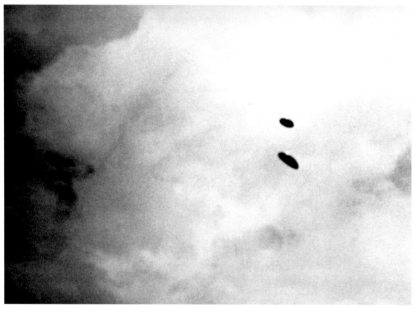

Wendelle C. Stevens and August C. Roberts. *UFO Photographs Around the World; Volume 1.* **Left top:** Photo by Rudi Nagora, p. 122. **Left middle:** Photo by Augusto Arronda, p. 63. **Left bottom:** Photo by Edilson Perez, 198. **Right:** Photo by Eduard J. Meier, p. 105.

Wendelle C. Stevens and August C. Roberts. *UFO Photographs Around the World; Volume 1.* **Left:** Photo by Sergio E. Schlimovich, p. 89. **Above:** Photos by George J. Stock, pp. 45 & 47.

Wendelle C. Stevens and August C. Roberts. *UFO Photographs Around the World; Volume 2.* **Left:** Photo by Domingo Troncoso, p. 135. **Right:** Photos by Harold Trudel, pp. 108 (top & middle) & 111 (bottom).

Wendelle C. Stevens and August C. Roberts. *UFO Photographs Around the World; Volume 2.* Photos by an anonymous photographer, pp. 28 (left top & bottom) & 29 (right top & bottom).

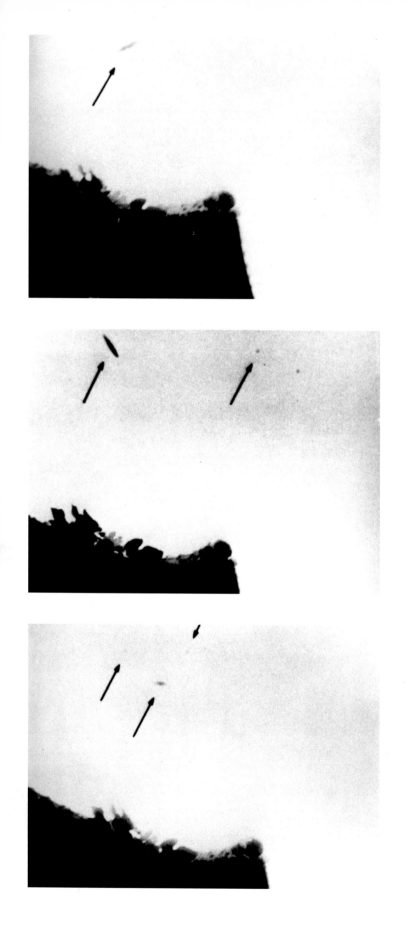

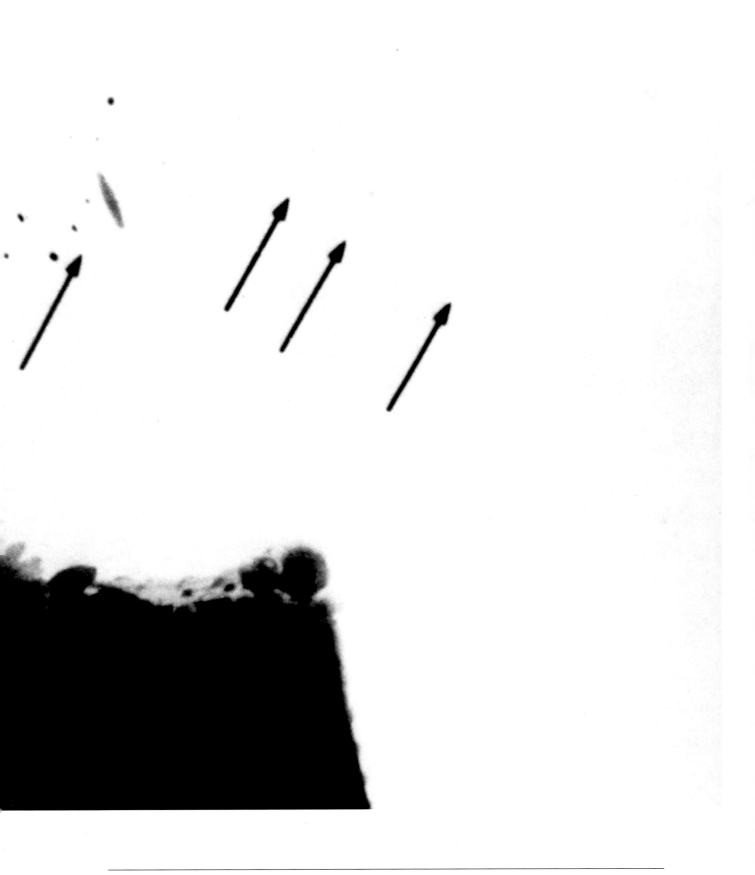

Wendelle C. Stevens and August C. Roberts. *UFO Photographs Around the World; Volume 2.* Photos by Hirohito Tanaka, pp. 80-81.

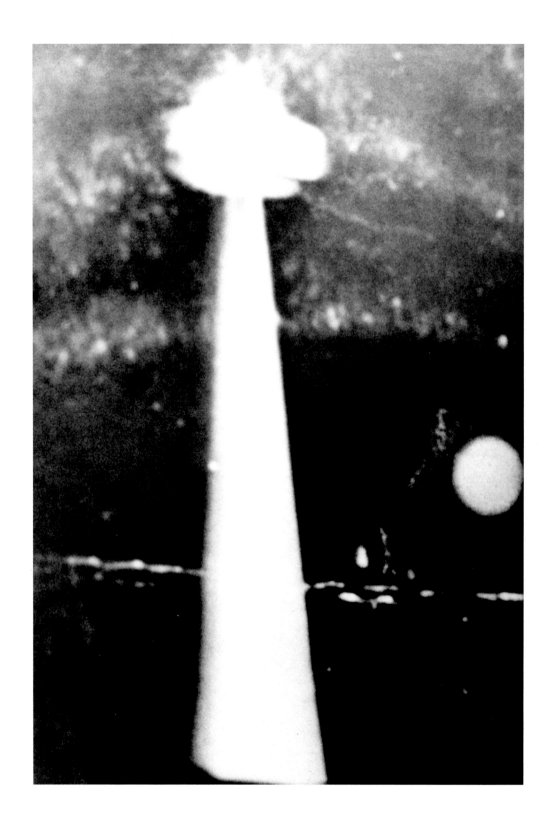

Wendelle C. Stevens and August C. Roberts. *UFO Photographs Around the World.* **Left:** Photo by an anonymous photographer, Volume 1, p. 206. **Right:** Photo by Tom O'Bannon, Volume 2, p. 187.

Wendelle C. Stevens and August C. Roberts. *UFO Photographs Around the World; Volume 2.* **Left top:** Photo by Helio Aguiar, p. 191. **Left bottom:** Photo by Tony Hartono, p. 210. **John Magor.** *Our UFO Visitors.* Saanichton, B.C., Toronto and Seattle. Hancock House, 1977. Hardcover book, imitation leatherbound with dust jacket. 264 p. Illustrated. **Right:** Photo from p. 141.

Wendelle C. Stevens and August C. Roberts. *UFO Photographs Around the World; Volume 1.* **Opposite:** Photo by an unidentified member of the Chilean Navy, p. 179. **Top left & bottom right:** Photos by Paulo Cernik, p. 147. **Top right:** Photo by David Mahon, p. 162. **Bottom left:** Photo by Dean Morgan, p. 175.

Wendelle C. Stevens and August C. Roberts. *UFO Photographs Around the World.* **Above and opposite bottom:** Photos by Eduard J. Meier, Volume 1, pp. 107 (above) & 108 (opposite bottom). **Opposite top:** Photo by James Bjornstad, Volume 2, p. 201.

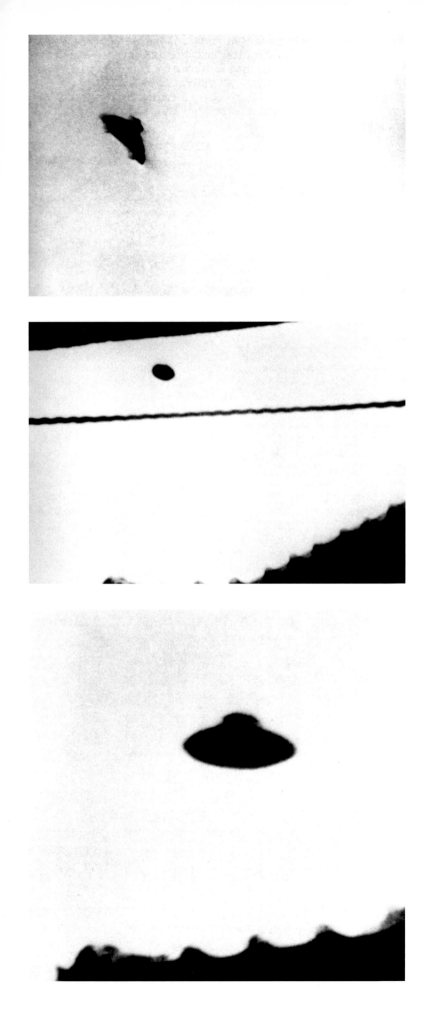

Wendelle C. Stevens and August C. Roberts. *UFO Photographs Around the World; Volume 1.* **Above:** Photo by Elizabeth Klarer, p. 74. **Left top:** Photo by Ryutaro Umehara, p. 165. **Wendelle C. Stevens and August C. Roberts.** *UFO Photographs Around the World; Volume 2.* **Left middle:** Hirohito Tanaka, p. 91. **Left bottom:** Hirohito Tanaka, p. 91.

FLYING SAUCERS FAREWELL

· · · · · · · · · · · ·

GEORGE ADAMSKI

Author of **INSIDE THE SPACE SHIPS**

ABELARD-SCHUMAN

OUT ON HIGHWAY 61

● ● ● ● ● ● ● ● ● ● ● ●

Polish-born George Adamski (1891–1965) arrived in Laguna Beach in the late 1930s, where he founded the Royal Order of Tibet. With one of his students, Mrs. Alice Wells, he purchased land on Palomar Mountain, on whose slopes he ran a roadside restaurant and where he claimed long after the fact to have seen a "mother ship" in 1946. Three years after, in 1949, he wrote and published the once-rare (now reprinted) *Pioneers of Space: A Trip to the Moon, Mars, and Venus*, offered to the public as science fiction. In 1952 he and several friends saw a saucer land in the nearby desert. After going off alone to investigate, Adamski claimed to have met a smiling young man with Nordic profile and Veronica Lake hair who had emerged from the craft. His "trousers were not like mine." Via telepathy, the man introduced himself as Orthon, from Venus, and they had a brief conversation.

With *Flying Saucer Review* co-founder Desmond Leslie, Adamski nominally co-wrote the bestselling *Flying Saucers Have Landed* (1953)—all of his books were, in fact, ghosted by Mrs. Wells and other students, and his Orthon-centered narrative incorporated material from his first book, though now presented as fact. In *Inside the Space Ships* (1955), he tells of trips taken with other space brothers, each one as lithe and blonde as the next whether they came from Venus, Mars, or Saturn; and of meeting Queen Juliana of the Netherlands. *Flying Saucers Farewell* (1961), however, sank without much trace. Ridiculed for claiming in 1962 to be attending a conference on Saturn, the following year he spread the word he'd had a secret meeting with Pope John XXIII. Those who knew him found it easier to believe he'd been to Saturn.

> People on Venus live hundreds of years in a single life span, then go through the experience we have named "death." To them it is but a moving out of one house that has served them well into another new house. The minerals of the body, having originated from their planet, are returned once again to the planet. Rather than mourning for the loss of a loved one, as is the custom on Earth, people on Venus rejoice in their loved one's opportunity to express through a new home somewhere in the Father's house of many mansions. Since there is no feeling of possession of one for another, there is no suffering due to separation, for the true love as understood by them knows no separation of any kind.

> — George Adamski, *Flying Saucers Farewell*, p. 91

George Adamski. *Flying Saucers Farewell.* London and New York: Abelard-Schuman, 1961. Clothbound with dust jacket. 190 p.

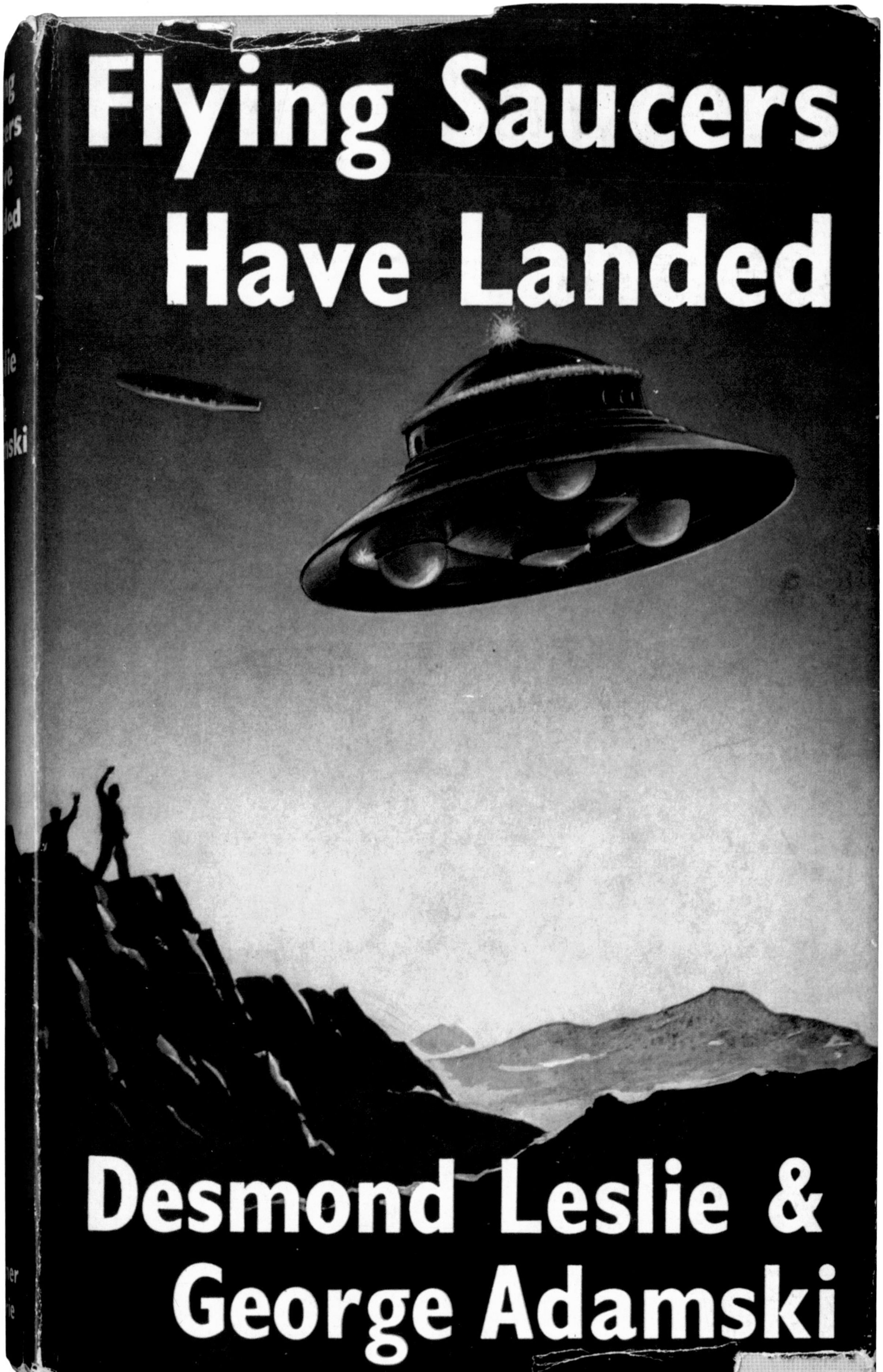

Flying Saucers Have Landed
Desmond Leslie & George Adamski

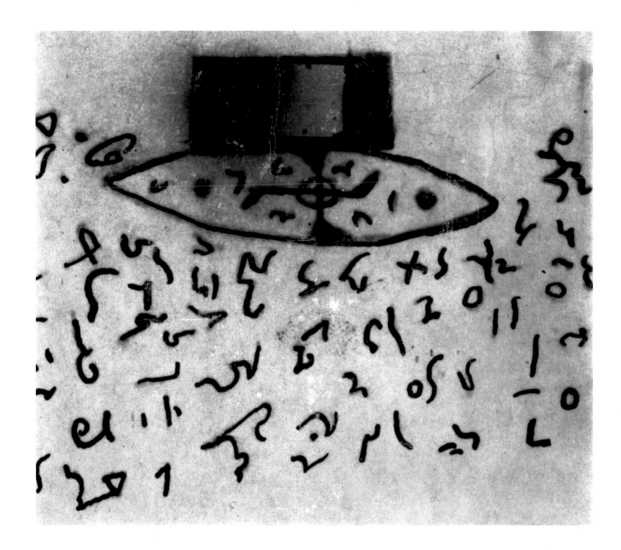

WRITINGS FROM ANOTHER PLANET

A brief technical account of flying saucers and their working method of propulsion.

This symbolic message, given to the authority by a visitor from outer space on December 13, 1952, has not been fully deciphered. Several scientists are working on it and on deciphering the markings of the footprints described in this book.

— *Flying Saucers Have Landed*, back cover

George Adamski and Desmond Leslie. *Flying Saucers Have Landed.* New York/London: The British Book Centre/Werner Laurie, 1953. Clothbound with dust jacket. 232 p. + 13 p. of plates. Illustrated. 3rd printing, Oct., 1953. **Left:** Front of jacket; **right:** back of jacket.

George Adamski and Desmond Leslie. *Flying Saucers Have Landed.* Plate opposite p. 49. **Opposite:**
Illustration from Wendelle C. Stevens and August C. Roberts. *UFO Photographs Around the World, Volume 2*, p. 184.

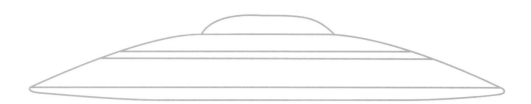

There were only two outstanding differences that I noticed as I neared him.

1. His trousers were not like mine. They were in style, much like ski trousers and with a passing thought I wondered why he wore such out here on the desert.

2. His hair was long, reaching to his shoulders, and was blowing in the wind as was mine. But this was not too strange for I have seen a number of men who wore their hair almost that long.

Although I did not understand the strange feeling that persisted, it was however a friendly feeling toward the smiling young man standing there waiting for me to reach him. And I continued walking toward him without the slightest fear.

Suddenly, as though a veil was removed from my mind, the feeling of caution left me so completely that I was no longer aware of my friends or whether they were observing me as they had been told to do. By this time we were quite close. He took four steps toward me, bringing us within arm's length of each other.

Now, for the first time I fully realised that I was in the presence of a man from space—A HUMAN BEING FROM ANOTHER WORLD! I had not seen his ship as I was walking toward him, nor did I look around for it now. I did not even think of his ship, and I was so stunned by this sudden realisation that I was speechless. My mind seemed to temporarily stop functioning.

The beauty of his form surpassed anything I had ever seen. And the pleasantness of his face freed me of all thought of my personal self.

I felt like a little child in the presence of one with great wisdom and much love, and I became very humble within myself … for from him was radiating a feeling of infinite understanding and kindness, with supreme humility.

To break this spell that had so overtaken me—and I am sure he recognised it for what it was—he extended his hand in a gesture toward shaking hands.

I responded in our customary manner.

— Leslie & Adamski, *The Flying Saucers Have Landed*, pp. 194–195

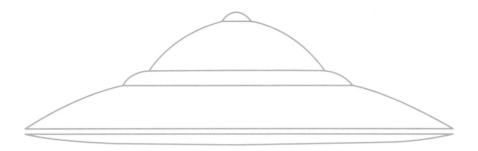

His questioning look seemed to ask if he had made the principle clearer.

Firkon, the Martian, spoke for the first time. "You understand the power of thought forms. Apart from our physical missions on Earth, all of us must hold firmly to the belief that the peoples of your Earth will themselves awaken to the disaster toward which they are moving."

"I see," I said slowly, as the issue did indeed clarify itself in my mind.

"We also are aware," Ilmuth pointed out, "as are you and many other people on your Earth, that your air forces and your governments *know* that our ships seen in your skies are coming from outer space, and that they can be made and piloted only by intelligent beings from other planets. Men high in the governments of your world have been contacted by us. Some are good men and do not want war. But even the good men on your Earth cannot entirely free themselves from the fear which has been fostered by man himself on your planet throughout the centuries."

"The same is true of your fliers everywhere on Earth," Kalna said quietly, "many have seen our ships again and again. But they have been muzzled and warned, and few dare speak out."

"It is the same with your scientists," Firkon added.

Again I marveled at their knowledge of our world and its peoples. "Then it would seem," I said, "that the answer lies largely with the ordinary man in the street, multiplied by his millions the world over."

"They would be your strength," Firkon quickly agreed, "and if they would speak against war in sufficient numbers everywhere, some leaders in different parts of your world would listen gladly."

— **George Adamski,** *Inside the Space Ships*, **pp. 99–100**

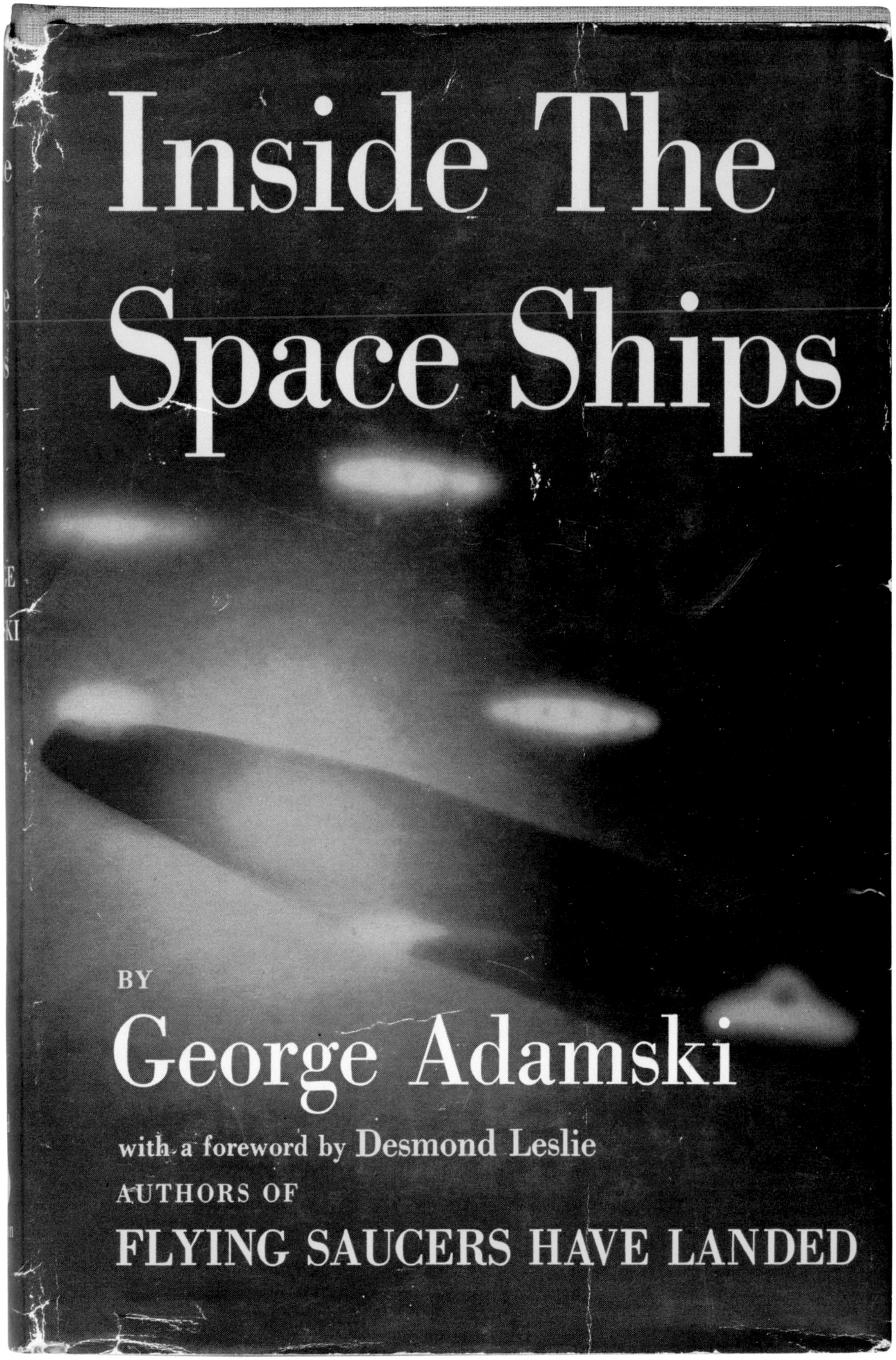

Inside The Space Ships

BY

George Adamski

with a foreword by Desmond Leslie

AUTHORS OF

FLYING SAUCERS HAVE LANDED

George Adamski. *Inside the Space Ships.* New York: Abelard-Schuman, 1955. Clothbound with dust jacket. 256 p. + 16 p. of plates. Illustrated. Signed by Adamski on front free endpaper. **Opposite:** Illustration from Wendelle C. Stevens and August C. Roberts. *UFO Photographs Around the World*, Volume 1, p. 96.

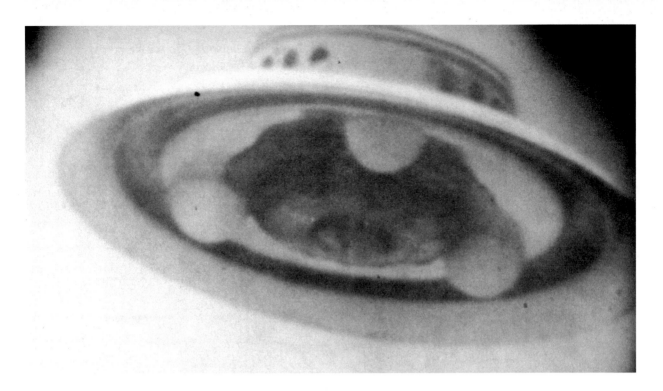

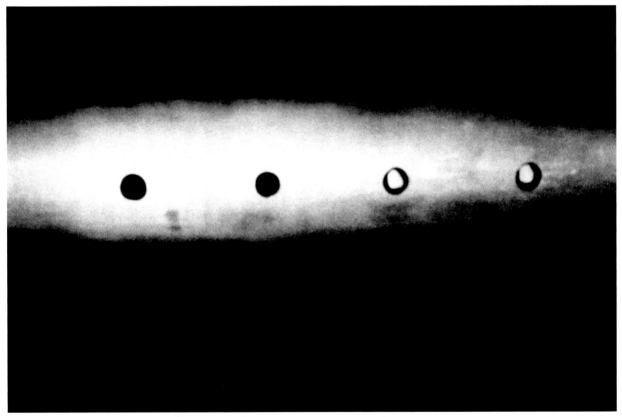

Above top: *Venusian Scout Hovering; A flying saucer–more precisely termed a Scout–photographed at 9 a.m. December 13, 1952 by George Adamski at Palomar Gardens, California through a six-inch telescope. Note a large magnifying lens and the three-sphered landing gear and the housing which contains the craft's main machinery underneath the ship.* From George Adamski, *Inside the Space Ships*, plate 6. **Above bottom:** *Portholes of a Small Mother Ship; A Venusian is at the first porthole, Adamski is at the second porthole in this second of the four photos.* From George Adamski, *Inside the Space Ships*, plate 13. **Opposite top:** *Diagram of Venusian Scout Ship.* From George Adamski, *Inside the Space Ships*, plate 2. **Opposite bottom:** *Diagram of Venusian Mother Ship.* From George Adamski, *Inside the Space Ships*, plate 3.

George Adamski. *Inside the Space Ships.*

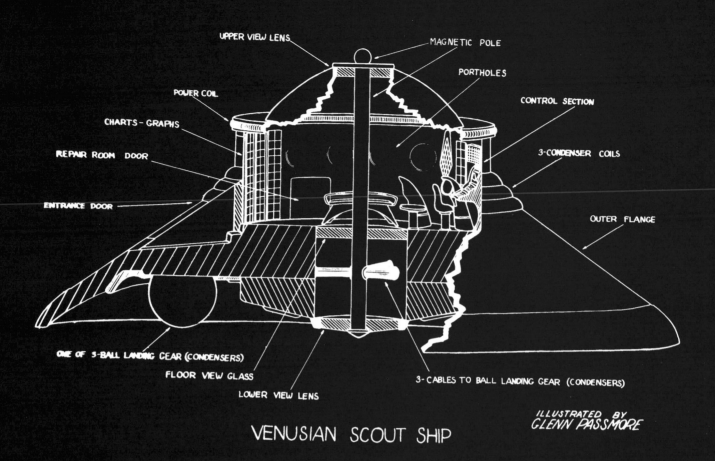

UPPER VIEW LENS   MAGNETIC POLE

POWER COIL   PORTHOLES

CHARTS - GRAPHS   CONTROL SECTION

REPAIR ROOM DOOR   3-CONDENSER COILS

ENTRANCE DOOR   OUTER FLANGE

ONE OF 3-BALL LANDING GEAR (CONDENSERS)

FLOOR VIEW GLASS

LOWER VIEW LENS

3-CABLES TO BALL LANDING GEAR (CONDENSERS)

ILLUSTRATED BY
GLENN PASSMORE

VENUSIAN SCOUT SHIP

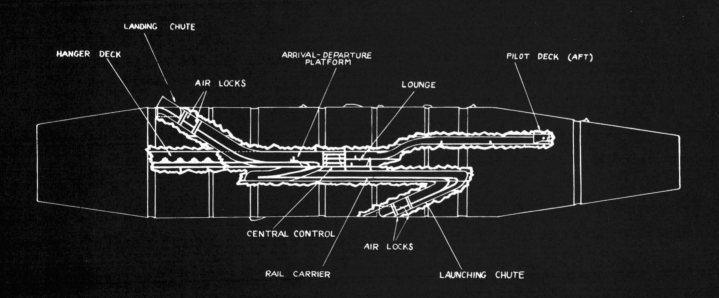

LANDING CHUTE

HANGER DECK   ARRIVAL-DEPARTURE PLATFORM   PILOT DECK (AFT)

AIR LOCKS   LOUNGE

CENTRAL CONTROL   AIR LOCKS

RAIL CARRIER   LAUNCHING CHUTE

ILLUSTRATED BY
GLENN PASSMORE

VENUSIAN SPACECRAFT
(MOTHER-SHIP)

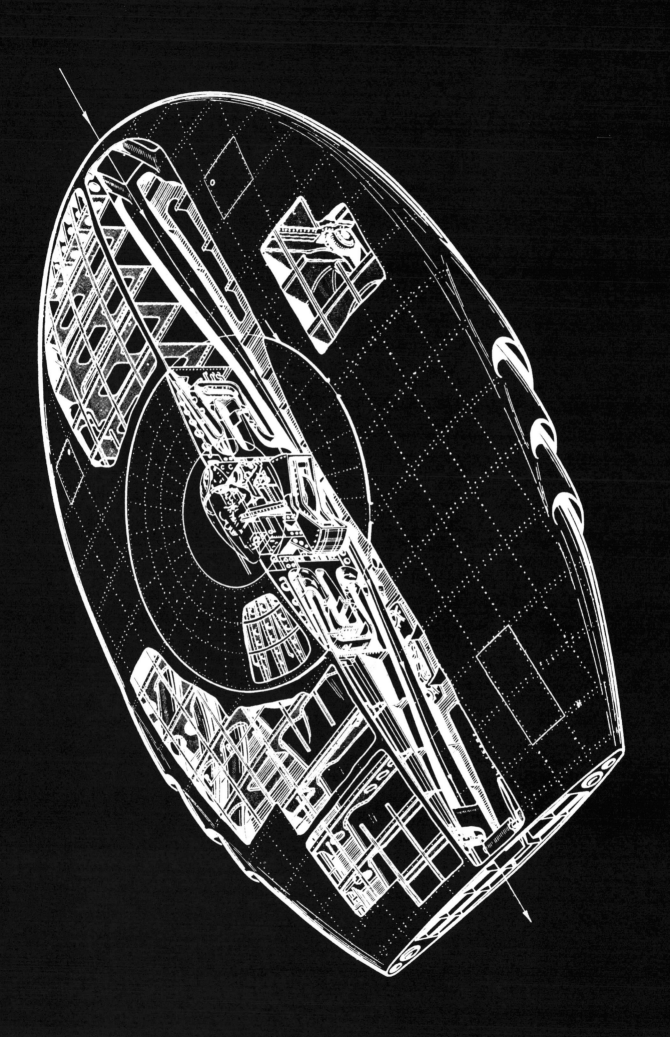

In his *Space, Gravity and the Flying Saucer* (1954), UK writer Leonard G. Cramp approached the subject not in the spirit of a believer, but an engineer (one nonetheless prone to repeatedly refer to the "ether"). He proposes that flying saucers are undoubtedly powered by an anti-gravity propulsion method similar to one of his own devising, and so examines at interminable length ways of getting around the key problem of neutralizing inertia. Cramp's astonishing schematic drawings of space ship interiors are eerily reminiscent of similarly-detailed Japanese anatomical charts of Gamera.

Leonard G. Cramp. *Space, Gravity & the Flying Saucer.* New York: British Book Centre, 1955. Clothbound with dust jacket. 182 p. + [4] p. of plates. Illustrated. Introduction by Desmond Leslie. **Opposite:** Interior design sketch from Cramp. Opposite illustration from p. 52.

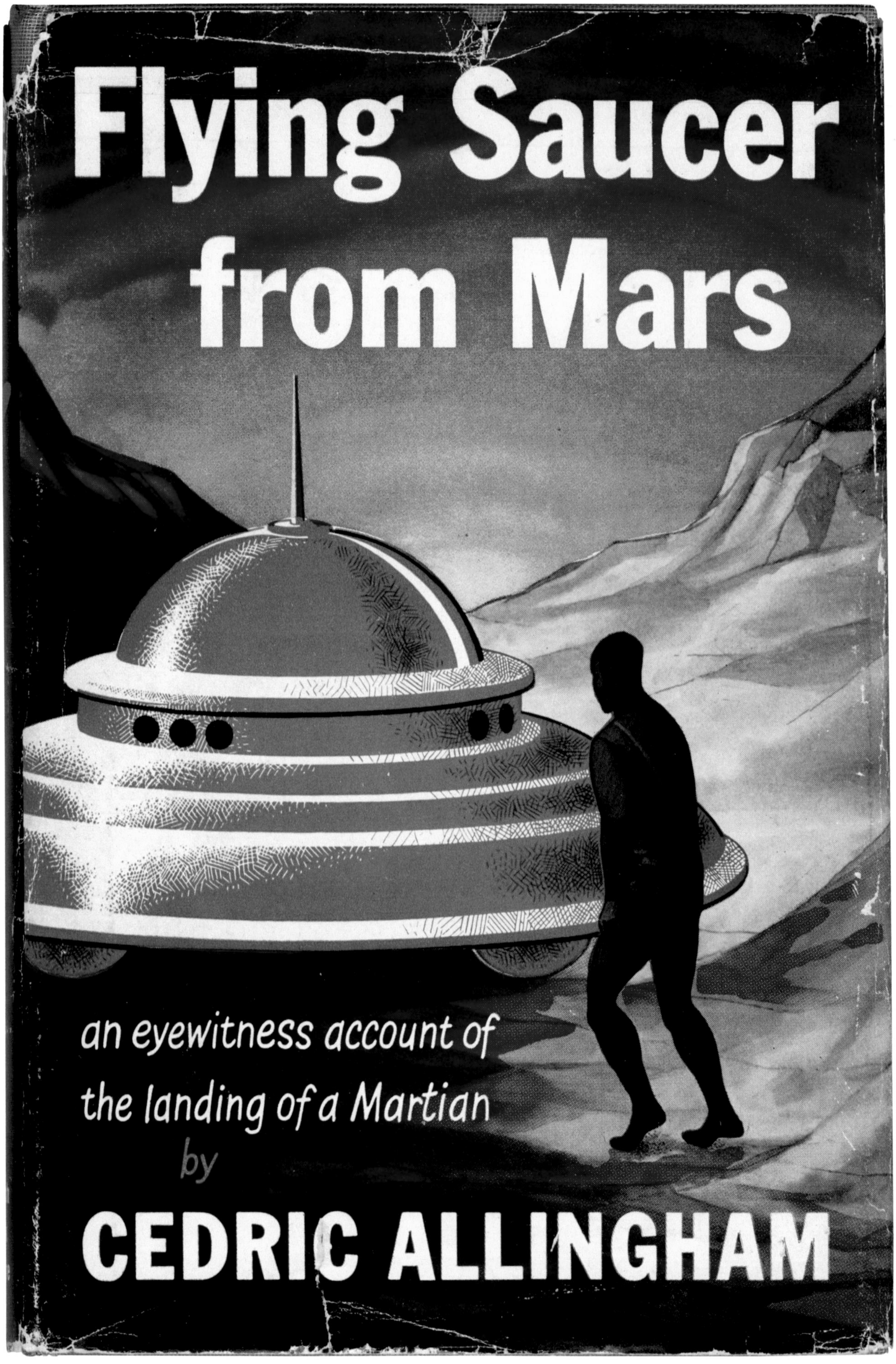

Flying Saucer from Mars

an eyewitness account of
the landing of a Martian
by

CEDRIC ALLINGHAM

The first of two photographs which the author took at approximately 3.45 p.m., as the Saucer was descending. The landing gear is clearly discernible to the lower left of the picture.

The non-existent Cedric Allingham claimed in *Flying Saucer From Mars* (1955) to have happened upon a craft and its pilot while on holiday. Via the traditional game of interplanetary telepathic charades "Allingham" ascertained the man was Martian, and returning from Venus. He offered as proof hazy photos of a man said to be the pilot standing with his back to the camera, gazing out over a fog-covered heath. Upon publication, British saucer clubs went to enormous lengths to draw the author out into public, being so persistent after a while as to cause his publisher to announce that he had gone to Switzerland, and died. The involvement of a well-known, recently deceased British astronomer in the writing of this wholly fraudulent account has been long hinted, but never confirmed. Peter Davies, a friend of the aforementioned astronomer, admitted in the mid-1980s to being one of the book's two authors, and also claimed to have at least once given a talk early on at a flying saucer club, posing as Allingham while wearing a false mustache.

Cedric Allingham (pseud.). *Flying Saucer from Mars.* New York: British Book Centre, 1955. Clothbound with dust jacket. 153 p. + [8] p. of plates. Illustrated. Subtitle on cover: "An eyewitness account of the landing of a Martian." **Above:** Plate 4.

Cedric Allingham (pseud.). *Flying Saucer from Mars.* Photo from back of jacket. **Opposite:** Illustration from Wendelle C. Stevens and August C. Roberts. UFO *Photographs Around the World, Volume 1*, p. 114.

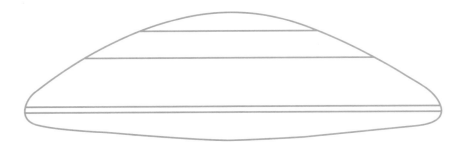

Cedric Allingham, born 1922 in Bombay, only son of a wealthy British textile manufacturer, was educated privately until he was ten, when his father retired and bought a house near Durban. Allingham's education was continued at schools in South Africa and England until he was seventeen when he entered a sanatorium with a serious illness which kept him on his back for nearly two years. In 1941 he joined the Army (RAOC) and was posted to the Middle East where he spent most of the war. It was during this time that he became interested in Astronomy through "identifying the stars for want of something better to do in the desert when it was too hot to sleep at night".

Since the war, and the tragic death of his parents, whose ship was torpedoed only nine weeks before the German surrender, Allingham has lived a nomadic life in a caravan in which he likes to travel the country, and in which he also makes long trips on the Continent. Most of his time is spent in writing thrillers (which he publishes under a pseudonym) and in bird-watching. He also owns a cottage in Yorkshire where he occasionally retires to do his "serious writing" and observe the moon and planets through his 10" reflecting telescope.

Since his unique experience, related in this book, he has started to make a collection of Flying Saucer sightings and is planning to carry out further extensive research during 1955 in California where a considerable number of Saucers have been reported seen in recent months.

— **Cedric Allingham, *Flying Saucer from Mars*, back cover**

George W. van Tassel. *Into This World and Out Again: A Modern Proof of the Origin of Humanity and its Retrogression From the Original Creation of Man. Verified by the Holy Bible. Revelations Received Through Thought Communication.* [N.p.: Privately published], 1956. Perfect bound in wrappers. 94 p. 1st ed. **Opposite:** Illustration from Wendelle C. Stevens and August C. Roberts. *UFO Photographs Around the World*, Volume 1, p. 91.

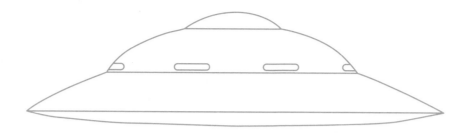

July 6, 1952.

"Salutations, My identity is Dulac, 411th projection, authority all waves, realms of Schare. Our center has directed me to throw the combined power of all waves under my authority to ray you a substance that will be very advantageous to your mortal being, your physical body. We are standing by 4300 miles above you, 742 in this projection. Our ray is now directed to you. Discontinue."

— George van Tassel, *I Rode a Flying Saucer*, p. 29

"Write the things <u>which</u> <u>thou</u> <u>hast</u> <u>seen</u>, and the things <u>which</u> <u>are</u>, and the things which shall be hereafter."

"'The New Jerusalem' referred to in the Bible, quoted in Rev. 21:10, is not really new. It is the positive polarity 'moon' that has been orbiting around the Earth for many thousands of years.

This satellite, called 'Shanchea' by our people, is a spacecraft. Our name for the Earth is 'Shan.' 'Chea' means child in our language of the Solex-Mal, or Solar Tongue. Therefore, the name of this ship is 'Earthchild' in English. This same craft was called 'The Star of Bethlehem' nineteen hundred and sixty years ago at the birth of the child called Jesus."

This is not new information. It has been before the eyes of Earthlings hundreds of years in print: though it was not recognized. Rev. 21:16 tells you, "And the city lieth foursquare, and the length is as large as the breadth: and he measured the city with the reed, twelve thousand furlongs. The length and the breadth and the height of it are equal."

— George van Tassel, *Into This World and Out Again*, p. 53

German immigrant Franz Critzer, a prospector, lived in rooms he'd dug out beneath the eponymous landmark on his California desert property, Giant Rock. Believed by locals after Pearl Harbor to be a Nazi spy, Critzer was accidentally blown up during a police siege in 1942 when his supply of dynamite was fired upon. After the cleanup, George Van Tassel (1910–1978) bought the property, building both a café and a dude ranch, expecting to lead a quiet life until the day he found himself astrally transported to meet the Council of Seven Lights. He is honest enough to note in his *I Rode A Flying Saucer* (1952) that he didn't actually ride a flying saucer, but the space brothers suggested that he give his work a more marketable title. He wrote other books, including *Into This World and Out Again* (1956), and from 1953 to 1978 he hosted as many as 10,000 saucer fans every year at the annual Giant Rock Saucer Convention.

In the late 1950s Van Tassel constructed a structure in Landers, CA he called the Integratron (designed by Venusians, funded in part by Howard Hughes) within which alien technology would rejuvenate the cell tissues of any human who stepped inside. After Van Tassel's death a proposal to turn the Integraton into a disco fell by the wayside.

George W. van Tassel. *I Rode a Flying Saucer! The Mystery of the Flying Saucers Revealed through George W. Van Tassel, Radioned to you by Other-World Intelligences in Reaction to Man's Destructive Action.* Los Angeles: New Age Publishing Co., 1952. Pamphlet in wrappers, saddle stapled. 51 p. 1 illustration. 2nd ed., revised and enlarged. **Above:** Photo from frontispiece.

I Rode a Flying Saucer

George W. Van Tassel

The Mystery of the Flying Saucers Revealed

The SECRET of the SAUCERS

By
ORFEO
ANGELUCCI

Here is an uplifting and in-spiring book — the true ac-count of a strange experi-ence with the visitors from outer space who act as our brothers and give us a mes-sage of hope.

Orfeo Angelucci (1912–1993) first saw the saucers and met their pilots on his daily commutes to and from the Lockheed plant in Burbank. The space brothers advised him on matters of life and philosophy, and once took him into earth orbit. It will likely not be surprising to know that after a lengthy correspondence with Angelucci, Ray Palmer published his book, *The Secret of the Saucers* (1955).

A blinding white beam flashed from the dome of the craft. Momentarily I seemed partially to lose consciousness. Everything expanded into a great shimmering white light. I seemed to be projected beyond Time and Space and was conscious only of light, Light, LIGHT! Orfeo, Earth, the past were as nothing, a dark dream of a moment. And that dream unfolded before my eyes in swift panorama. Every event of my life upon Earth was crystal clear to me—*and then memory of all my previous lives upon Earth returned.* IN THAT SUBLIME MOMENT I KNEW THE MYSTERY OF LIFE! Also, I realized with a terrible certainty that we are all—each one of us—TRAPPED IN ETERNITY and ALLOTTED ONLY ONE BRIEF AWARENESS AT A TIME!

— Orfeo Angelucci, *The Secret of the Saucers*, p. 34

Although one may contact you in absolute silence and be invisible to your physical sight, some moment in the future you may have a "spiritual awakening," when you will remember the saucer's vigil. The awakening may be years after the actual contact was in effect. It seems the extra-terrestrials really "favor" such persons by keeping them entirely undisturbed by visual experiences. Today these millions of persons are those who *know* space visitors are here. They do not know how they know it, but they accept it anyway. Most have never seen a saucer knowingly or have caught only an uncertain glimpse of one. But for them the day is coming when through extra-dimensional perception, they will "remember" and their eyes will be opened. Several of the finest contacts to date are of this nature.

— Orfeo Angelucci, *The Secret of the Saucers*, pp. 152–153

Orfeo Angelucci. *The Secret of the Saucers.* [Amherst, WI]: The Amherst Press, 1955. Clothbound with dust jacket. xiv, 167 p. Edited by Ray Palmer.

This SPACE CRAFT, or As Affectionately Called By
Her Woman Captain AURA RHANES Our Admiral SCOW
Was Entered Into By TRUMAN BETHURUM, Who Therein,
Spoke To The Captain And Her 32 Member Male Crew.

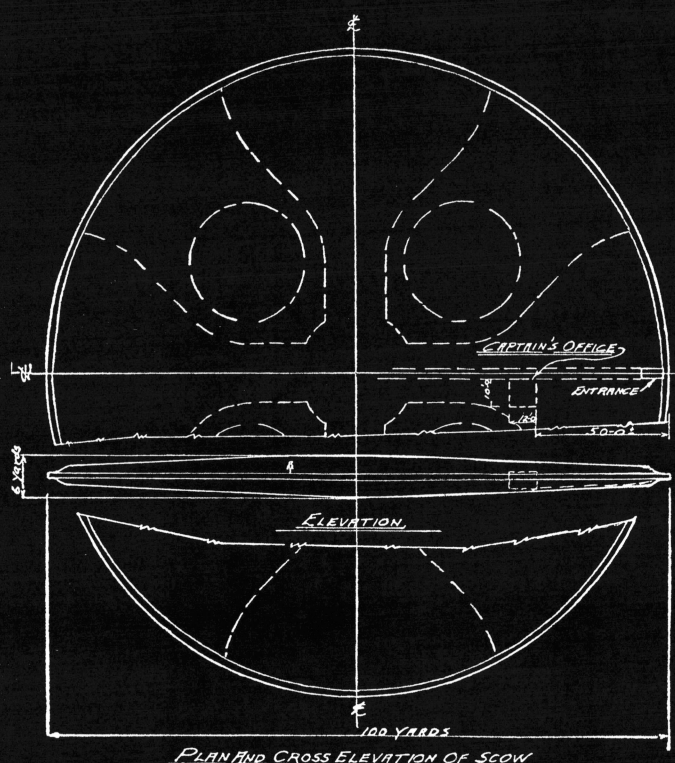

PLAN AND CROSS ELEVATION OF SCOW
—— SCALE ⅛" TO YARD   Drawn by O.B. Lavbie

Road grader by day, spiritual advisor by night, Truman Bethurum (1898–1969) wrote in *Aboard A Flying Saucer* (1954) of meeting a flying saucer crew and their beautiful captain, Aura Rhanes (her uniform mostly Paris New Look and topped with a fetching beret). They came from the planet Clarion, which eternally remains invisible from earth, being blocked from our view by the moon–Bethurum wisely tries not to explain how this is possible. He was one of the era's more popular contacts; after he and his second wife divorced (her jealousy of Captain Rhanes seemingly an issue) he married his third at the Giant Rock Spacecraft Convention.

Truman Bethurum. *Aboard a Flying Saucer.* Los Angeles: DeVorss & Co., 1954. Clothbound with dust jacket. 192 p. Illustrated. **Opposite:** Illustration from frontispiece.

Truman Bethurum. *Aboard a Flying Saucer.* **Above:** Photo from back cover.

ABOARD A FLYING SAUCER

By TRUMAN BETHURUM

This extraordinary book written by Truman Bethurum contains an exact account of his experience with the Admiral Scow, generally known by us as a Flying Saucer.

Mr. Bethurum describes this huge "Saucer" in great detail as to size, shape, kind of metal used and construction in general. He also obtained valuable information regarding the means of propulsion, which we believe has never been told before.

During his eleven visits with the Captain of the saucer, he discussed many things with her, such as the location and name of their home planet and their way of life. Many, many interesting and enlightening facts are brought out that hitherto were unknown.

Don't miss this true, exciting narrative of an "out-of-this-world" adventure covering a period of several months.

— *Aboard a Flying Saucer*, dust jacket flap

I had written to my wife again, telling her more about the saucers from Clarion and their woman captain, even though she had practically forbidden me to ever mention them again. It is easy to see that I was obsessed by the visits of these people, and that I wanted my wife to know all about them and if possible to meet them too. [...]

Instead of answering this letter, Mary telephoned, and finally got me on the line at the Desert Inn at Overton, Nevada. Her first words to me, after greeting me, were as emphatic as my letter had been.

"Truman," she said, "I don't like these letters you've been writing me. Of course, I want to get letters from you, but I told you several times that I don't want to hear any more about those weird things you've been writing to me. I've come to the conclusion that you're just trying to make me jealous, through all this mention of hours talking with some beautiful space woman, so you can get me up there. Well, it won't work. I'm not jealous. And I'm not coming up there in all that heat."

— Truman Bethurum, *Aboard a Flying Saucer*, p. 128

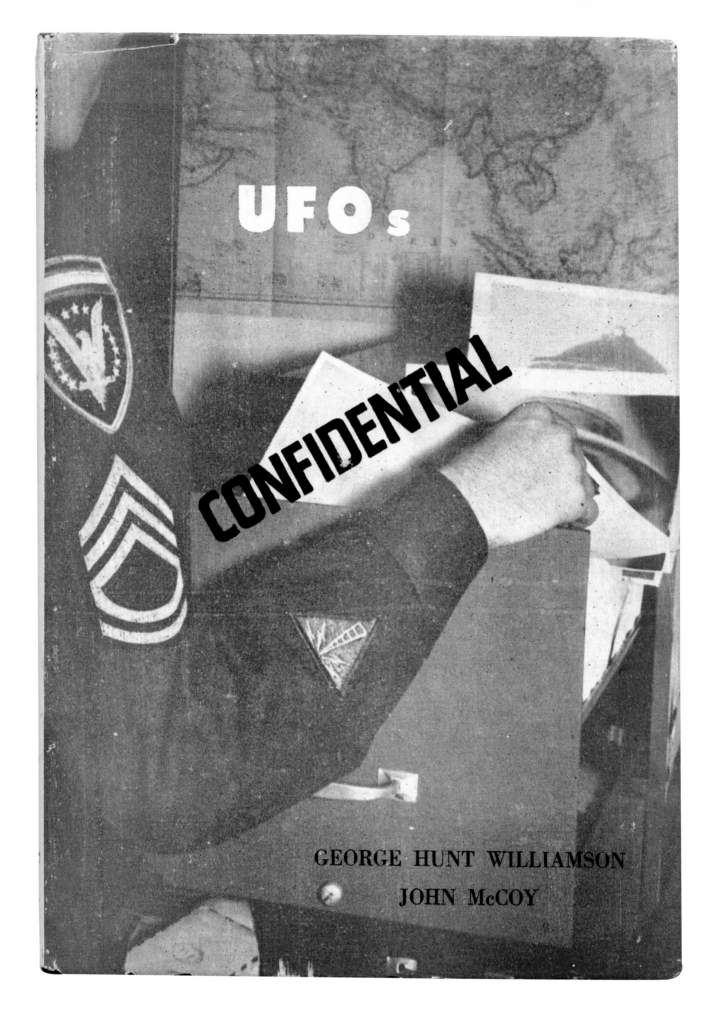

UFOs

CONFIDENTIAL

GEORGE HUNT WILLIAMSON

JOHN McCOY

When George Adamski set out across the desert to meet Orthon at his space ship, George Hunt Williamson (1926–1986) and his wife were present, and later claimed to have also seen the ship land. They remained close supporters and friends until Williamson began receiving his own messages from the space brothers via a Ouija board of his own creation—an act of betrayal in Adamski's eyes. In *The Saucers Speak* (1954) Williamson presented his Ouija transcriptions as shortwave radio communications with pilots of the flying discs; the pilots went by such monikers such as Artok, of Pluto. Following the publication of *UFOs Confidential* (1958), Williamson withdrew from active participation in the saucer world, though he continued to turn out such works as *Other Tongues, Other Flesh* (1957) which borrow heavily from Theosophical concepts and teachings, along with healthy doses of far less savory beliefs.

17 August 1952, 8.25 p.m.

"I am Zo. I am head of a Masar contact group, but my home is Neptune. I am going to Pluto soon. Pluto is not the cold, dreary world your astronomers picture it to be. Mercury is not a hot, dry world, either. If you understood magnetism you would then see why all planets have almost the same temperatures regardless of distance from great Sun body. Sister rites are Universal rites. They are rotting. Earth is backward, too many wars. Peace to all men everywhere."

"Regga speaking. Please put water on your stove to boil. It will help our contacting you at this time."

"Zo again. 'To apples we salt, we return.' You may not understand this strange saying now, but someday you will. It is from one of our old prophecy legends. Rites will save your people. We are here to warn you. If there is dissension amongst you we will not contact you. Be calm and quiet!"

— **George Hunt Williamson,** *The Saucers Speak*, **pp. 51–52**

George Hunt Williamson and John McCoy. *UFOs Confidential! The Meaning Behind the Most Closely Guarded Secret of All Time.* [Corpus Christi, TX: Essene Press], 1958. Clothbound with dust jacket. 100 p.

George Hunt Williamson. *The Saucers Speak: A Documentary Report on Interstellar Communication and Radiotelegraphy.* London: Neville Spearman, 1963. Clothbound with dust jacket. 160 p. Illustrated. First British edition; originally published: Los Angeles: New Age Publishing Company, 1954.

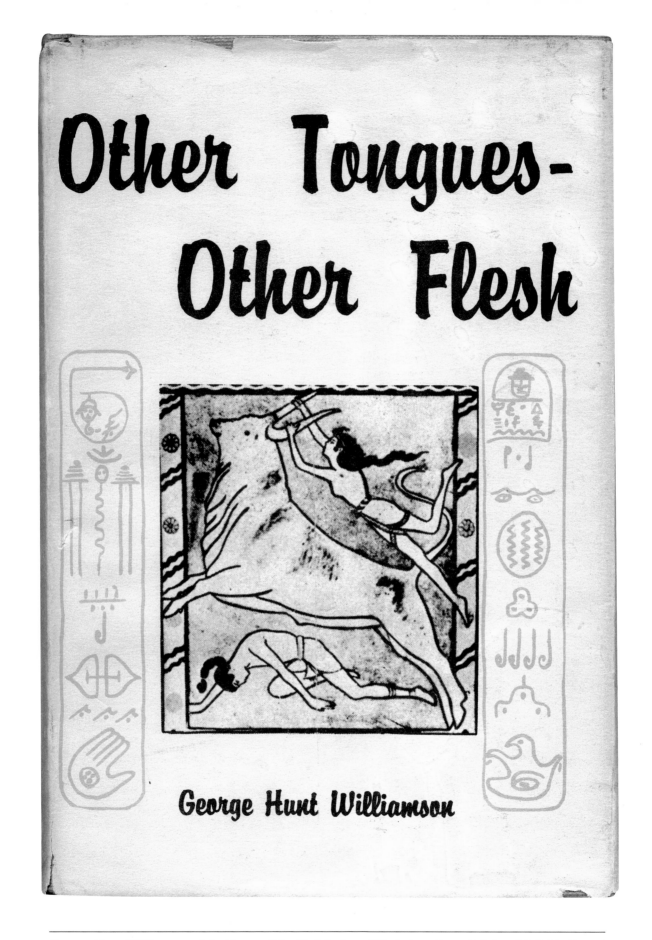

George Hunt Williamson. *Other Tongues–Other Flesh.* Amherst, WI: Amherst Press, 1953 [i.e. 1957?]. Clothbound with dust jacket. 448 p. Illustrated.

Some UK writers brought a wide-eyed if not overly creative spirit to the field. Journalist Gavin Gibbons retold the stories of Adamski, Bethrum, and others in his two books, *The Coming of the Space Ships* (1958) and *They Rode in Space Ships* (1957), managing to make their accounts far less interesting.

The sceptic will at once rub his hands together with glee and claim that by debunking George King and the other four stories, I have cut the ground from underneath my feet. But before being so triumphant, he should remember Tony Roestenberg and George Adamski. Just as these two men are telling the truth, so I believe the veracity of Daniel Fry and Truman Bethurum.

— **Gavin Gibbons,** *They Rode in Space Ships*, **p. xix**

Gavin Gibbons. *They Rode in Spaceships: Fantastic Meetings with Spacemen.* London: Neville Spearman, 1957. Clothbound with dust jacket. xx, 217 p. + [4] p. of plates. Illustrated. **Gavin Gibbons.** *The Coming of the Space Ships.* New York: The Citadel Press, 1958. Hardcover book, clothbound with dust jacket. viii, 188 p. + [4] p. of plates. Illustrated. First American edition; originally published by Neville Spearman in 1956. **Opposite:** Photo from frontispiece.

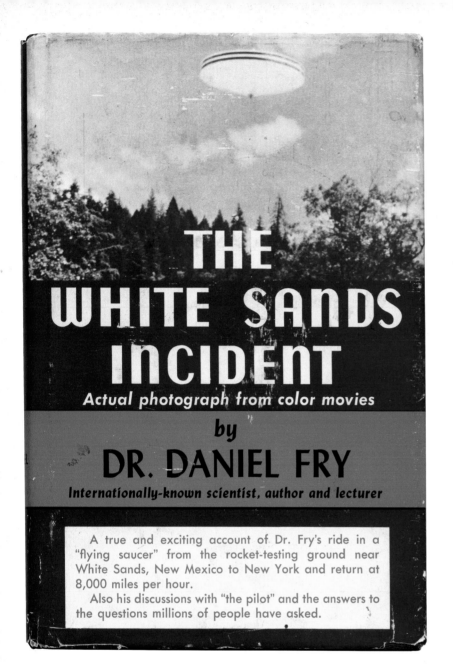

THE **WHITE SANDS INCIDENT**

Actual photograph from color movies

by

DR. DANIEL FRY

Internationally-known scientist, author and lecturer

A true and exciting account of Dr. Fry's ride in a "flying saucer" from the rocket-testing ground near White Sands, New Mexico to New York and return at 8,000 miles per hour.

Also his discussions with "the pilot" and the answers to the questions millions of people have asked.

Daniel Fry (1908–1992) was walking in the New Mexico desert when he found his path blocked by an oblate spheroid. "Better not touch the hull, pal, it's hot," warned the pilot, Alan (pronounced A-LAWN), over an unseen speaker. Invited aboard, Fry rode to and from New Mexico to New York City in half an hour while Alan pontificated on physics and world peace. Soon after writing *The White Sands Incident* (1954), Fry failed a lie detector test. Didn't stop him.

"To New York—and back—in thirty minutes!" I said. "That's eight thousand miles per hour! How can you produce energies of that order on a craft like this, and how can I stand the acceleration? You don't even have seat belts on these seats!"

— **Daniel Fry**, *The White Sands Incident*, **p. 33**

Daniel W. Fry. *The White Sands Incident.* Louisville, KY: Best Books Inc., 1966. Clothbound with dust jacket. 120 p. Illustrated. Second edition; originally published: Los Angeles: New Age Publishing Co., 1954. **Opposite:** Illustration from plate opposite p. 31.

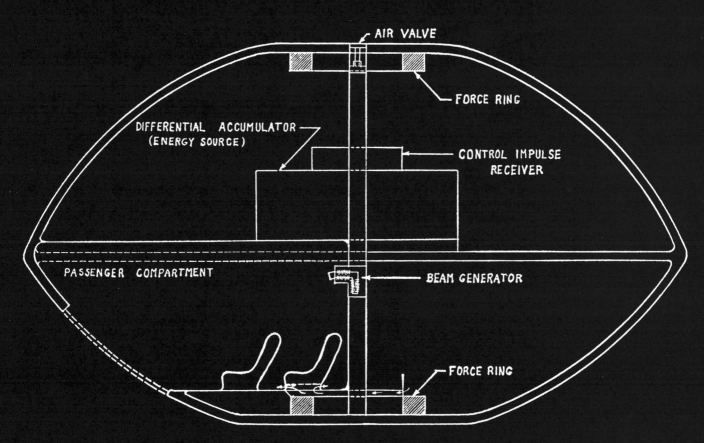

INSIDE OF SPACE SHIP DESCRIBED BY DANIEL FRY, PH.D.

FLYING
SAUCERS
CLOSE UP

JOHN W. DEAN

A GROUND SCOOTER USED ON THE MOON
FROM A DRAWING BY ROBERT RENAUD.   RENDERED BY JOHN DEAN.

SPACEMEN URGED THE AUTHOR
TO COMPILE THIS BOOK, SUPPLIED
MUCH OF THE INFORMATION AND
APPROVED THE WORK

Flying Saucers Close Up (1969) by John W. Dean, is perhaps the ultimate Saucerian Books title. A hefty folio, the cover illustration and space brothers' imprimatur "SPACE MEN URGED THE AUTHOR TO COMPILE THIS BOOK, SUPPLIED MUCH OF THE INFORMATION AND APPROVED THE WORK" says all that needs saying. Some of the material is also found in his earlier title, *Flying Saucers and the Scriptures*, but here the refinements of his theories are clear.

I have little reason to believe that this country, or any other, will give up its warring and corruption, its grafting and greed, in order to be fit to join the Alliance and save itself from depravity and total loss. I think those citizens unfortunate enough to be living then will see a similarity to the biblical prediction of the taking away of the Holy Spirit. These space enemies may be the demons or the "powers and principalities" spoken of, but we will have to fight against their "flesh and blood" representatives. And if they are the Kalrans, it will be over in five minutes! The way our government has opposed and rejected the assistance offered by the local planets during the early days, and that of the friendly Korendians more recently, indicates that it will give in to Kalran domination in hope of saving itself. I do not believe that the "take-over" by friend or foe will preserve any nation as a separate unit.

We once had a presidential candidate who talked much about a "one world government," but I paid little attention to him. I wonder now, if he was influenced by spacemen having similar ideas. If so, I should have listened to him then. I wonder if Alf Landon is still available.

— John W. Dean, *Flying Saucers Close Up*, p. 24

I have been asked many times why I am willing to devote so much time and effort to the study of space matters—the people, their ships, their work and their play. Could it be that somewhere in my subconscious mind, too deep for me to realize it, there are memories of a previous life on a better world? Or is it only a thorough disgust with what I have seen develop here in USsia after two useless wars when we were told in Phony War 1 that we were fighting to make it a world fit to live in—with everlasting peace? "A war to end all war."

— John W. Dean, *Flying Saucers Close Up*, p. 192

John W. Dean. *Flying Saucers Close Up*. Clarksburg, WV: Gray Barker, 1969/1970. Perfect bound in wrappers. 224 p. Illustrated.

A REMOTELY CONTROLLED RECORDER DISC
APPARENTLY PHOTOGRAPHING A FLOAT IN THE
ROSE PARADE IN PASADENA, JANUARY 1, 1953.
THIS PICTURE WAS TAKEN BY CARL FIRMIN.

John W. Dean. *Flying Saucers Close Up.* **Opposite top:** p. 19. **Opposite bottom:** p. 22. **Top:** p. 45.

En route to the 1956 Giant Rock saucer convention, Bryant and Helen Reeve set out interviewing contactees they met along the way: Adamski, Truman Bethrum, George Williamson, Daniel Fry, Orfeo Angelluci, and George Van Tassel. It becomes clear enough to the reader of *Flying Saucer Pilgrimage* (1957) very quickly that the focus of the book is not in fact on cut-and-dried retellings of now-familiar stories, but rather a full report on and appreciation of medium Mark Probert, who channels the members of the Inner Circle of the Cosmic Council (not to be confused with the Council of the Seven Lights or similar such bodies). Note the cover's use of the Arnold saucer illustration, ten years after the fact.

After we had met many a saucerer [...] we were truly appalled by one thing. That was what the public expects of a saucerer!

It is like this. Some decent, honest, self-respecting chap is going someplace, or is just sitting someplace minding his own business. Then down comes a saucer—and bang! All of a sudden he is a genius. In a flash he is supposed to know everything. Overnight he is catapulted into prominence. He suddenly becomes a somebody, even if that somebody is only a target for ridicule and the butt of many a joke. His friends hear about his experience, and they all start asking him questions. They ask this question and that question and some in-between questions. They amuse themselves at his expense. [...]

The public expects just about everything of a saucerer. They expect him to be a combination of a modern cosmic Galileo, Columbus, Einstein, Kinsey and Messiah—all from a few minutes saucer experience. They expect him to know all about everything, including such minor items as the planets, the galaxies, the ethers, outer-space, energy, static-electricity, magnetism, cosmology, space-ship technology, metallurgy and instrumentation, extra-terrestrial science, sociology, agriculture, education, religion, government, living conditions on Mars, the latest fashions on Venus, the sexual behavior of Plutonians, and real estate and business opportunities on the asteroids!

— **Bryant and Helen Reeve,** *Flying Saucer Pilgrimage,* **pp. 147–148**

Bryant & Helen Reeve. *Flying Saucer Pilgrimage.* Amherst, WI: Amherst Press, 1957. Clothbound with dust jacket. 304 p. Illustrated.

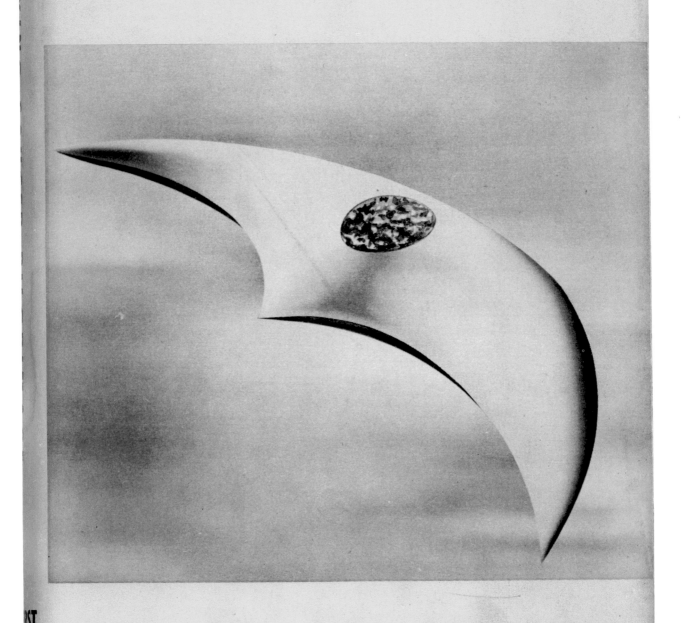

Flying Saucer
Pilgrimage

Bryant & Helen Reeve

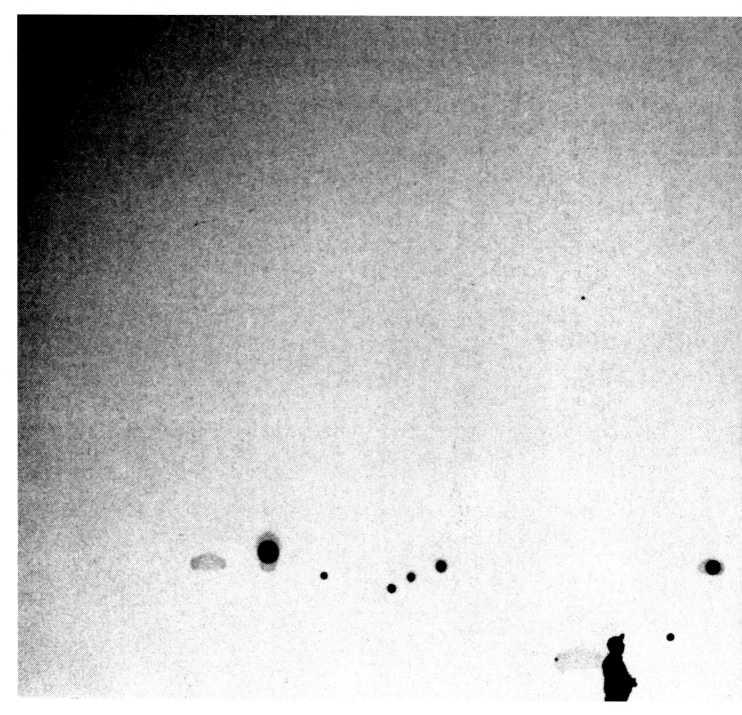

The Author in a UFO Shower

Trevor James. *They Live in the Sky.* Los Angeles: New Age Publishing Co., 1958. Clothbound with dust jacket. 270 p. + [32] p. of plates. Illustrated. **Above:** Plate [30].

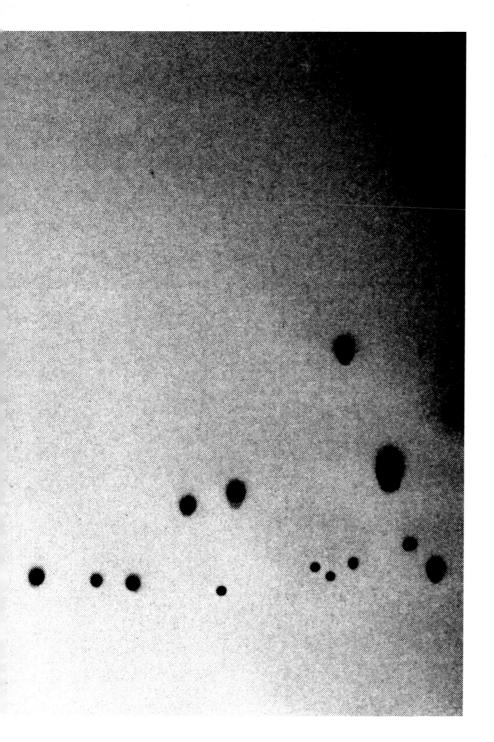

In California today we have a group of young women "receptors" who have gone around impressing their friends with complacent statements about being used for "tests" and "wonderful experiments" with the "space people." Tests and experiments of this type usually reach the point where even the feelings of these women are under unseen control, and "space" craft land, disgorging giant entities who bang on midnight doors.

One must resolve to keep all such unsavory invisibles out of one's life and personal world, even if the "penalty" be no communication at all. The prize is the security of one's own temple, beside which the reception of trash from the invisibles is not to be compared.

— Trevor James, *They Live in the Sky!*, p. 166

Trevor James [Constable], who in earlier years worked the Cloudbuster apparatus for Wilhelm Reich, spent lengthy periods of time in the California deserts taking infrared photos, thereafter examining the developed film for images of what he called "critters," that is to say enormous flying amoebas of demonstrable intelligence. In *They Live in the Sky!* (1958) he suggests such critters might propel themselves with Reich's proposed energy, Orgone, and have become visible to humanity since the war, thanks to radar.

Trevor James. *They Live in the Sky.* **Above:** "UFO Ahoy," plate [26].

They Live in the Sky!

in the Sky!

By Trevor James

Invisible Incredible UFO Around Us

Former flight attendant Gloria Lee (1925–1962) channeled messages from an entity on Jupiter called JW, who appeared–judging from the examples included in *Why We Are Here!* (1962) to obtain his material exclusively from the Ray Palmer publication *Oahpse*. In a development worthy of Nathanael West, at JW's direction Gloria Lee undertook a hunger strike to draw world attention to her plan for world peace. No one noticed, and after 66 days she starved to death.

Gloria Lee. *Why We Are Here: By J.W., a Being from Jupiter, Through the Instrumentation of Gloria Lee.* Los Angeles: DeVorss & Co., 1959. Clothbound with dust jacket. 183 p. Illustrated. **Opposite:** Photo from back of jacket. **Following pages:** Illustrations and text from pp. 20 & 72.

We shall land quickly. Be with us in love. If you wait for us to come to you first, the time will be short. You will have to be rushed to meet the schedule we have set up. But if you should come to meet us, we can land before you reach our landing spot. You must wait until we tell you to approach our ships! The ships we fly are surrounded by a magnetic field of force which could injure you if you come to us before we tell you it is safe.

Wait for us to land and then wait for our instructions. We shall tell you when to come aboard. Pack a small bag when you see us and we will not have to wait for you to be ready. We cannot wait for you to return to your homes to prepare. That would take too much time. When we can, we'll let you know before hand so you shall be able to prepare. The plan is, we shall announce this intention of action by your radios and televisions and even to some people, by telephone. It is possible for us to intervene on your instruments.

— Gloria Lee, *Why We Are Here!*, p. 140

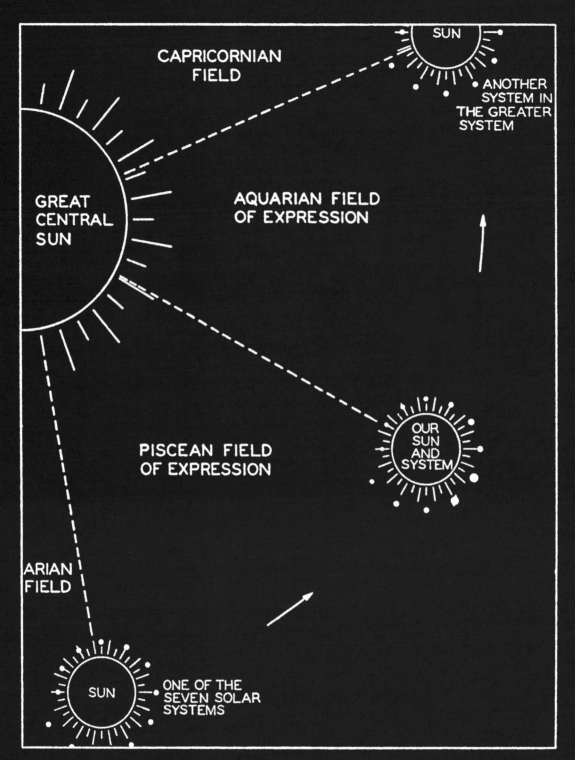

It requires a year for our planet *earth* to revolve around our sun accompanying the other planets within our system, traveling at their own particular rate of revolution. At the same time, our solar system, as a unit, revolves around the great Central sun billions of miles away. All seven of the systems in the Greater System revolve together.

Just as our year is divided into twelve parts, the times and *areas* around the Central Sun are divided into twelve parts. Each period is a little over 2100 years and the time to complete the circle is 26000 years.

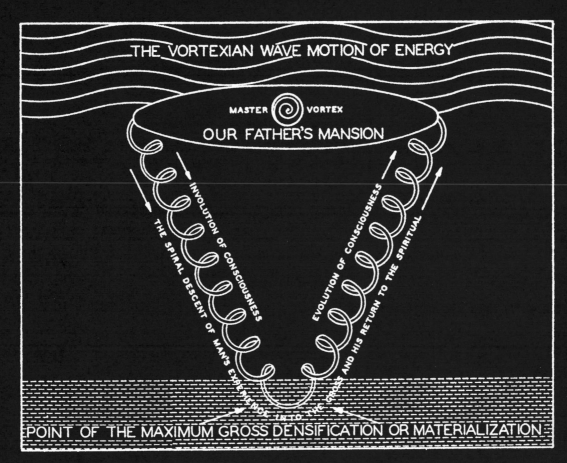

By clairvoyantly observing electricity flowing through a wire, one could see the *spiral* flow of energy. Many researchers have concluded all energy travels in spirals. Thus the cosmic energy or spiritual force which sustains and flows through man, follows the same pattern throughout the omniverse.

This diagram represents the descent or involution of Spirit (man) into matter, reaching the lowest, or *maximum* gross point of materialization and gathering the chaff of human experience. *The Soul* awakens, and seeks the path Home, with the help of his evolved consciousness. Thus an individual makes many rounds of experience as he progresses through descent and ascent. The story of the Prodigal Son also represents involution and evolution. There can be no evolution without involution. Life operates in cycles.

Form dominates the period of Involution and Spirit (or ability to change form at will as there is no true form other than that which is needed to operate in) dominates Evolution of the higher planes. Thus, the Space People in their higher evolvement can *change* their form as explained in chapter II. Form really *imprisons* Spirit.

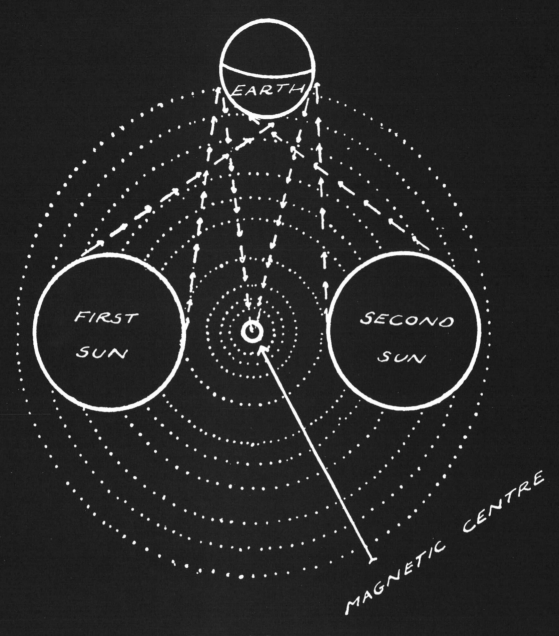

FIG. 4. A BINARY SYSTEM.

The entry of a new Sun into our system would throw the Earth out into an orbit between Mars and Jupiter now occupied by the planetoids. All the planetary orbits will be altered. There will be turmoil, but this will be bearable as the repulsive force of the new Sun will speedily restore order. When the new Sun reaches it maximum luminosity the Earth will already be in its appointed place in the system. There will certainly be a change in the fauna, but life will continue, probably under better conditions than before.

The entry of this new body into the system was predicted by Nostradamus in his famous *Centuries*, vol. II, stanza 41:

"La grande estoile par sept jours bruslera
Nuee fera deux soleils apparoir."

(The great star will burn for seven days, and cloud will
make two Suns appear.)

"Dino Kraspedon" was the pseudonym of Brazilian Aladino Felix, arrested in his country in 1968 on suspicion of terrorist activity. In *Flying Saucers* he claims to have met a saucer commander who discussed physics, and social justice.

The author's sincere thanks go to the Captain of the Flying Saucer, whether he be from Space, from Earth or from below the Earth, for the confidence and understanding which he showed on so many occasions; for overlooking our mistrust; and for never refusing to answer our questions, though he could have had no personal interest in mankind other than to give a little of himself in the hope that we should become better people, knowing all the while that his efforts would probably go unrewarded.

— Dino Kraspedon, *My Contact With Flying Saucers*, p. 5

Dino Kraspedon (pseud. of Aladino Felix). *My Contact with Flying Saucers.* London: Neville Spearman, 1959 (6th printing, 1973). Clothbound with dust jacket. 205 p. Illustrated. Translated from the Portuguese by J.B. Wood. **Opposite:** Illustration from p. 54.

FROM
OUTER SPACE
TO YOU

by HOWARD MENGER

An account of visitors from space
...documented by actual photographs

"We'll be seeing you!"

At age ten, New Jerseyan Howard Menger (1922–2009) met his first alien, a beautiful blonde woman sitting on a rock. Later, after the war, he found himself in regular contact with men and women claiming otherworldly origins. He helped them move freely through earth life; they took him to the moon and let him hold a space potato. In 1956 he met Connie Weber, who he perceived to be the reincarnation of the Space Sister he'd met long before. Three years later he wrote *From Outer Space To You*, where among much else he tells of serving as Barber to the Space People, and why graham flour is good for digestion. (When the book was republished in paperback in the 1960s, the revised title left it at FROM OUTER SPACE.) Howard and Connie had two children and were married for over fifty years. Selections from his *Authentic Music From Another Planet* are readily findable on YouTube.

Howard Menger. *From Outer Space to You.* Clarksburg, WV: Saucerian Books, 1959. Clothbound with dust jacket. 256 p. + [16] p. of plates. Illustrated. **Above:** Photo from plate following p. 256.

"Sit down and play it, the melody," he offered, gesturing toward the instrument, but I stammered the only thing I could play was a phonograph. He put his hand on my shoulder and spoke reassuringly.

"*This* music you can play, Howard," and he guided me gently toward the chair in front of the "piano." I sat, protestingly.

"From this time on you will be able to play a piano whenever you are moved to do so, and not only this tune, but any melody you wish."

I looked down at the keyboard. It was entirely different from a conventional piano keyboard. This one was much longer and contained many more keys, which were narrower and had strange symbols on them which I did not understand. The entire instrument was much lower and closer to the floor.

I almost automatically reached down to touch the keys, suddenly knowing which to strike to correspond with the sounds of the melody running through my mind. Although I had never been able to play before, it all seemed natural and delightfully simple.

— **Howard Menger, *From Outer Space To You*,**
pp. 117–118

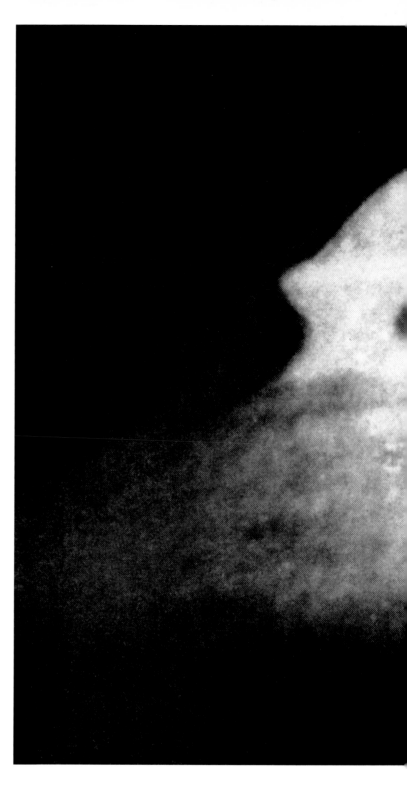

Howard Menger. *From Outer Space to You.* **Above:** Photo from plate opposite p. 33.

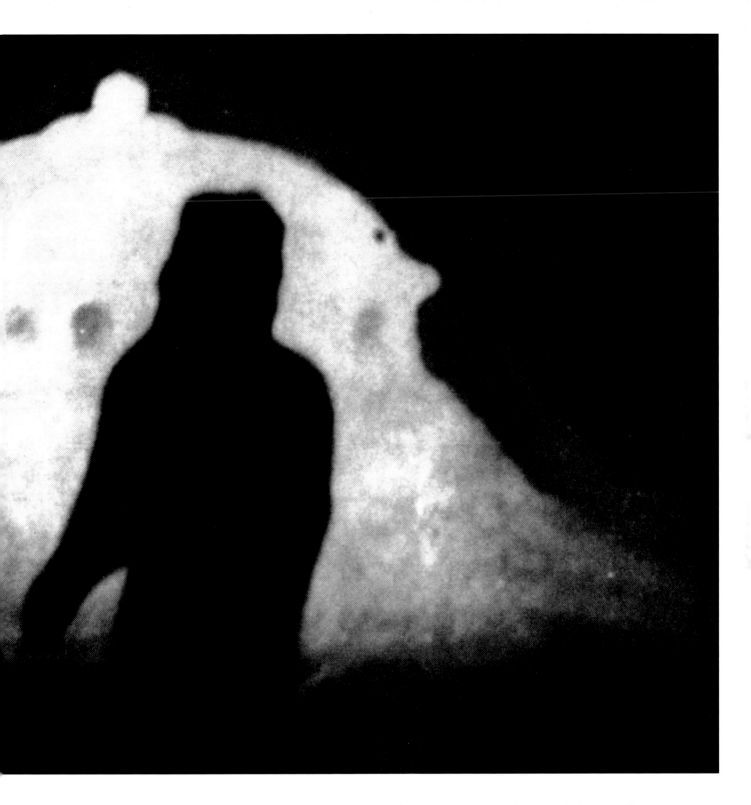

Venusian man allows the author to photograph him in silhouette against background of lighted spacecraft. Space people are reluctant to permit clear photographs of their features, because they might be recognized while mingling with Earth people. An aura or force field can be seen around spacecraft in original photograph, but much detail is lost in printing process.

BRAND NEW Enlarged Edition
Latest, Up-to-the-minute FACTS on UFO!

THE REPORT ON
Unidentified
Flying Objects

Edward J. Ruppelt

Former Head of the United States Air Force Project Blue Book

Investigating Flying Saucers

STOP WATCHING THE SKIES

● ● ● ● ● ● ● ● ● ● ●

The US Air Force opened Project Saucer (later Project Grudge and ultimately, Project Blue Book) in 1948 to deal with public inquiries regarding UFOs. By all accounts director Edward Ruppelt (1923–1960), initially regarded saucers with an open mind. The first edition of his *The Report on Unidentified Flying Objects* (1956) concludes that some sightings did remain unexplained and, accordingly, the subject was worthy of further investigation. Soon after, Keyhoe asked Ruppelt to serve as a NICAP adviser, but after feeling too much pressure from the former he declined. Ruppelt then spent time investigating the world of the "contactees," such as Adamski *et al.* Three additional chapters appeared in the book's second edition; Ruppelt's new conclusion was that further study of the subject in any way would be a complete waste of time. He died of a heart attack that same year, age 37.

A lieutenant colonel who had been sitting quietly by interjected a well-chosen comment. "It seems the difficulty that Project Blue Book faces is what to accept and what not to accept as proof."

The colonel had hit the proverbial nail on its proverbial head.

— **Edward Ruppelt,** *The Report on Unidentified Flying Objects* **(revised edition), p. 195**

The only reason there are any "unknowns" in the UFO files is that an effort is made to be scientific in making evaluations. And being scientific doesn't allow for any educated assuming of missing data or the passing of judgment on the character of the observer. However, this is closely akin to being forced to follow the Marquis of Queensbury rules in a fight with a hood. The investigation of any UFO sighting is an inexact science at the very best. Any UFO investigator, after a few months of being steeped in UFO lore and allowed a few scientific rabbit punches, can make the best of the "unknowns" look like a piece of well-holed Swiss cheese.

— **Edward Ruppelt,** *The Report on Unidentified Flying Objects* **(revised edition), p. 277**

Edward J. Ruppelt. *The Report on Unidentified Flying Objects.* Garden City, NY: Doubleday & Company, Inc., 1956. Clothbound with dust jacket. 277 p. Revised edition.

32. In the following sketch, imagine that you are at the point shown. Place an "A" on the curved line to show how high the object was above the horizon (skyline) when you *first* saw it. Place a "B" on the *same* curved line to show how high the object was above the horizon (skyline) when you *last* saw it.

33. In the following larger sketch place an "A" at the position the object was when you *first* saw it, and a "B" at its position when you *last* saw it. Refer to smaller sketch as an example of how to complete the larger sketch.

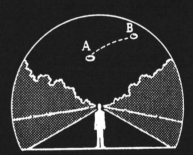

USAF Public Information Officer Lawrence J. Tacker's 1960 report, *Flying Saucers and the US Air Force*, has a magnificent cover but otherwise made little impression on either believers or deniers.

Lawrence J. Tacker. *Flying Saucers and the U.S. Air Force.* Princeton, NJ: D. Van Nostrand Company, Inc., 1960. Clothbound with dust jacket. xi, 164 p. Illustrated. **Opposite:** Illustration from p. 104.

Myth-Truth-History

Flying Saucers

DONALD H. MENZEL
Professor of Astrophysics

*A Great
Astronomer
explains the facts*

Donald H. Menzel. *Flying Saucers.* Cambridge, MA: Harvard University Press, 1953. Clothbound with dust jacket. xii, 319 p. Illustrated.

Harvard astronomer Dr. Donald Menzel (1901–1976) and *Flying Saucers* (1953) were to the field of saucerology what Dr. Frederick Wertham and his book *Seduction of the Innocent* (1954) were to the world of comic books—the difference being that Dr. Menzel's work was grounded entirely in fact, and the illustrations were not nearly so distracting.

The Arnold story was scarcely 24 hours old before the hoaxers, jokers, and publicity seekers of the nation moved in. The subject matter lent itself admirably to such activities. People had seen saucers in the sky. People wanted to see more. And so the jokers started tossing wheel-shaped objects of all sorts and descriptions from the tops of the tallest buildings. These activities produced the desired result. The women screamed, as they are supposed to on such occasions. The men—at least after they realized that the object would not explode—bravely picked it up and showed its true nature. Everyone had a good laugh. And the newspapers had a field day.

— **Donald Menzel, *Flying Saucers*, p. 39**

Why, then, have so many civilized people chosen to adopt an uncivilized attitude toward the flying saucers? I think there are three reasons.

First, flying saucers are unusual. All of us are used to regularity. We naturally attribute mystery to the unusual.

Second, we are all nervous. We live in a world that has suddenly become hostile. We have unleashed forces we cannot control; many persons fear we are heading toward a war that will destroy us.

Third, people are enjoying this fright to some extent. They seem to be a part of an exciting piece of science fiction.

Such analysis, however, is more the province of the psychologist than of the natural scientist. Let us, then, hasten back to our flying saucers. In our role of scientific detective we may examine the steps of reasoning that have led so many to accept the interplanetary concept. Is there any flaw in their argument? And if so, can we turn it to advantage and employ the arguments as an aid to further understanding of the saucers themselves?

— **Donald Menzel, *Flying Saucers*, p. 53**

In 1966 the US Air Force funded the University of Colorado UFO Project, a committee under the direction of one-time Manhattan Project physicist Edward Condon, designated to examine all of Project Blue Book's saucer reports along with those held by NICAP and others, as well as all sightings reported during the eighteen-month life of the project. Their conclusion appeared in 1969 in *Scientific Study of Unidentified Flying Objects*. The verdict: Further studies of the subject are unlikely to yield scientific discoveries.

Thus ended science's semi-formal interest in UFOs as well as the interest of major media of the time—network TV, *Life*, *Time*, and the rest. Apollo 11 landed on the moon that same year, and the final remnants of romance clinging to the subject of space travel, that longtime dream of the 20th century—encompassing the canals of Mars, the moon bases, the jungles of Venus—dropped away as well. Popular science, science fiction, and saucerdom all suffered accordingly, and profoundly.

> Our general conclusion is that nothing has come from the study of UFOs in the past 21 years that has added to scientific knowledge. Careful consideration of the record as it is available to us leads us to conclude that further extensive study of UFOs probably cannot be justified in the expectation that science will be advanced thereby.

> — **Edward U. Condon,** *Scientific Study of Unidentified Flying Objects*, **p. 1**

> The question remains as to what, if anything, the federal government should do with the UFO reports it receives from the general public. We are inclined to think that nothing should be done with them in the expectation that they are going to contribute to the advance of science.

> This question is inseparable from the question of the national defense interest of these reports. The history of the past 21 years has repeatedly led Air Force officers to the conclusion that none of the things seen, or thought to have been seen, which pass by the name of UFO reports, constituted any hazard or threat to national security.

> — **Edward U. Condon,** *Scientific Study of Unidentified Flying Objects*, **p. 4**

Edward U. Condon. *Final Report of the Scientific Study of Unidentified Flying Objects: Conducted by the University of Colorado Under Contract to the United States Air Force.* New York: E.P. Dutton & Co., Inc., published in association with Colorado Associated University Press, 1969. Clothbound with dust jacket. xxiv, 967 p. + [32] p. of plates. Illustrated.

Scientific Study of Unidentified Flying Objects

The complete report on the study conducted by the University of Colorado under research contract number F44620-67-C-0035 with the U.S. Air Force

Dr. Edward U. Condon
University of Colorado, Project Director

Introduction by
Walter Sullivan
of
The New York Times

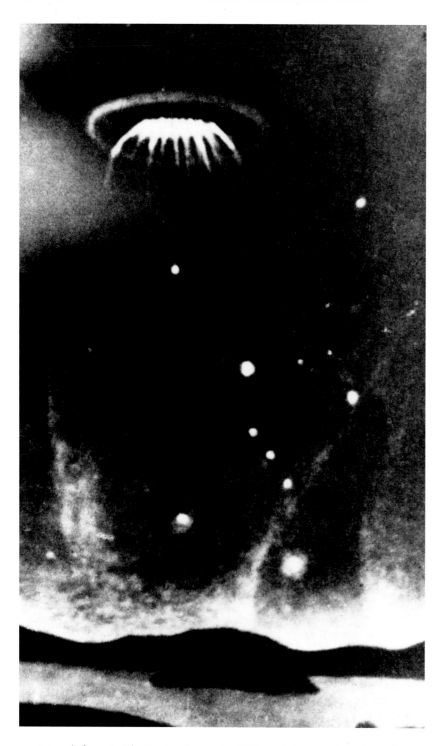

James Oberg, perhaps best known for his *Red Star In Orbit*, one of the earliest studies in English of cover-ups within the Soviet space system, later wrote *UFOs and Outer Space Mysteries* (1982); again employing elegant common sense in dealing with the subject at hand, again arriving at the same conclusions, and again enjoying similar sales as other such skeptical works.

Artwork from inside Russia shows the UFO and its tentacles above the constellation Orion. Courtesy of Coleman Von Keviczky

---

James E. Oberg. *UFOs & Outer Space Mysteries: A Sympathetic Skeptic's Report.* Norfolk and Virginia Beach, VA: Donning, 1982. Perfect bound in wrappers. 192 p. Illustrated. **Above:** Photograph from p. 165.

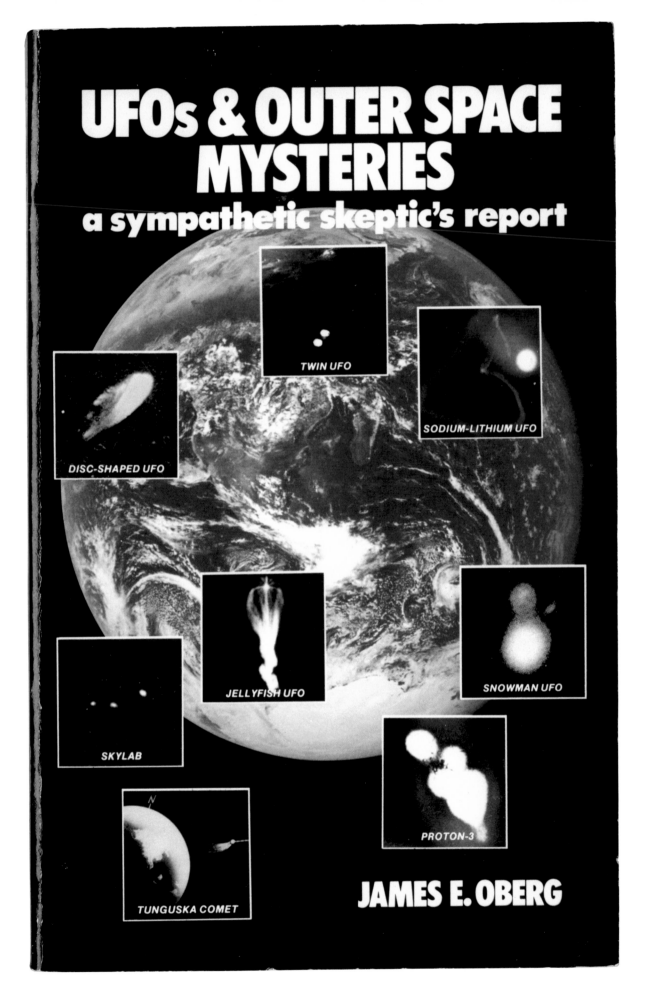

UFOs & OUTER SPACE MYSTERIES

a sympathetic skeptic's report

TWIN UFO

SODIUM-LITHIUM UFO

DISC-SHAPED UFO

JELLYFISH UFO

SNOWMAN UFO

SKYLAB

PROTON-3

TUNGUSKA COMET

JAMES E. OBERG

FLYING SAUCERS

MYTHS

MADNESS OR

MADE IN MOSCOW?

Don Boys, D. D.

Boys, Don. *Flying Saucers: Myths, Madness, or Made in Moscow?* Scotia, NY: Arcturus Book Service, 1982. Pamphlet in wrappers, saddle stapled. 81 p. Illustrated. Reprint; originally published: Indianapolis, Ind.: Goodhope Press, [n.d.].

MOON IN THE SEVENTH HOUSE, JUPITER COLLIDING WITH MARS

● ● ● ● ● ● ● ● ● ● ● ● ●

By the end of the 1950s popular interest in flying saucers waned, subsumed to some degree within the greater if more inchoate panic that followed the launching of Sputnik. By early 1964, when the sixties were really starting to get going, there came renewed worldwide interest in all things paranormal, including flying saucers, more often now called UFOs.

Noted evangelist W.V. Grant, Sr., was the author of such classic tracts as *I Was A Cannibal*, and father of televangelist W.V. Grant, Jr. (convicted of tax evasion in 1996, was later head pastor of the Eagles' Nest Cathedral Church in Dallas). His private theory was readily adaptable when it came to UFOs.

As the New Age fully took hold, along with rants from the pulpit on other dangers (see: *Communism, Hypnotism, and the Beatles*) there was no shortage of warnings on the dangers of flying saucers. A typical example: *Flying Saucers: Myths, Madness, or Made in Moscow?* (ca. 1960s–1970s, reprinted 1982). Its text is as timeless as any collection of 17th century sermons re: Wonders in the Sky.

Many other Ufologists believe that the flying saucers have come to earth to show us the way to true brotherhood and peace. They will give us cures for cancer and the common cold. They will give us plans for machines that will make our greatest achievements look like the work of retarded children. A few people profess to have seen UFOs on the desert and had conversations with these preachers of peace and prosperity. They tell us if we will only listen to them our world will be free of war, crime, disease, poverty, and sorrow. But the Bible warns us of believing in this social gospel preached from the desert and backed with great miracles. Luke 24:24-26 says, "For there shall arise false Christs, and false prophets, and shall shew great signs and wonders; insomuch that, if it were possible, they shall deceive the very elect. Behold, I have told you therefore. Wherefore if they shall say unto you, Behold, he is in the desert; go not forth…" These people are false prophets, and we are told not to believe them.

— **Don Boys, *Flying Saucers: Myths, Madness, or Made in Moscow?*,**
pp. 10–11

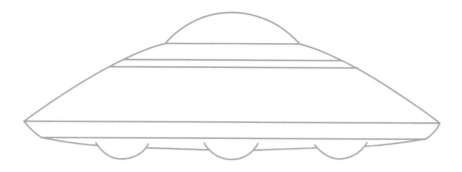

4. How Can These Men Be So Deceived?

One of them I talked with recently was a student of a man from Tibet, who brings his students into a frame of mind, so they can't tell where they are in the body or out. They go on long trips in the air as they go off into trances. They get revelations from the spirit world. While they are out in space—believing they are in their bodies up there—they see, hear, and talk with "space men" (demons). They imagine that they can walk through closed doors, with the "space men".

The word, luna, means the moon and the god of the moon. Thousands of people worship the moon. They claim there is supernatural power there. The word, Lunar, is used in referring to the moon. The word, lunatic is given to people who are possessed with evil spirits. Devil possessed people act worse during the full moon. It is no wonder that Satan has his headquarters near the moon, and that Russia is racing to beat us there!

These men say the planet, Lucifer, was destroyed by atom bombs. Read again in Isaiah 14:12-17 and you will see that the devil is afraid of the judgments of God, afraid he will be destroyed again. That is why he is worried.

These men who contact the supernatural spirits do so during the full moon, for that is when they seem to work best. It was in the new moon that the heathen people worshiped [sic] their gods (Hosea 2:10—11).

— Evangelist W.V. Grant, *Men from the Moon in America*, p. 24

W.V. Grant. *Men From the Moon in America: Did They Come in a Russian Satellite?* Dallas, TX: Rev. W.V. Grant. [1950s–60s]. Pamphlet in wrappers, saddle stapled. 31 p. **Opposite:** Illustration from Wendelle C. Stevens and August C. Roberts. *UFO Photographs Around the World*, Volume 2, p. 186.

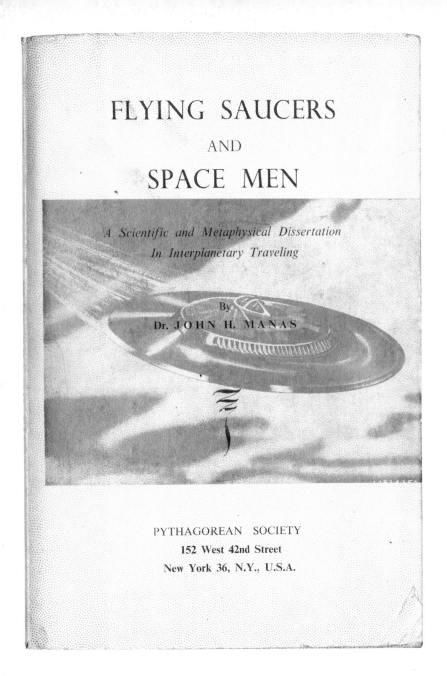

FLYING SAUCERS

AND

SPACE MEN

A Scientific and Metaphysical Dissertation
In Interplanetary Traveling

By
Dr. JOHN H. MANAS

PYTHAGOREAN SOCIETY
152 West 42nd Street
New York 36, N.Y., U.S.A.

Meade Layne (1882–1961) and other noted metaphysicians of the California school such as the Pythagorean Society's Dr. John H. Manas (*Flying Saucers and Space Men*, 1962), proposed an interdimensional origin for the saucers, be it either the fourth dimension, or what Layne called the Etheric Zone.

We know that the spiritual atmosphere of our Earth has a thickness of approximately 4,331 miles. If we accept the theory that the spiritual atmosphere of Venus has the same thickness, then the distance of separation of these two planets from the spiritual plane of the other, will be approximately 24,690,000 miles, which will occur once in every 584 days at the inferior synodical period of Venus. If we accept the belief that any communication of spiritual entities can ever be possible between these two planets of our solar system, then the only propitious time would be once in every 584 days, at the inferior conjunction of Venus and not every day of the year.

— **John H. Manas,** *Flying Saucers and Space Men*, **p. 75**

John H. Manas. *Flying Saucers and Space Men: A Scientific and Metaphysical Dissertation in Interplanetary Traveling.* New York: Pythagorean Society, 1962. Perfect bound in wrappers, with dust jacket. 124 p. Illustrated. **Opposite:** Illustration from p. 47.

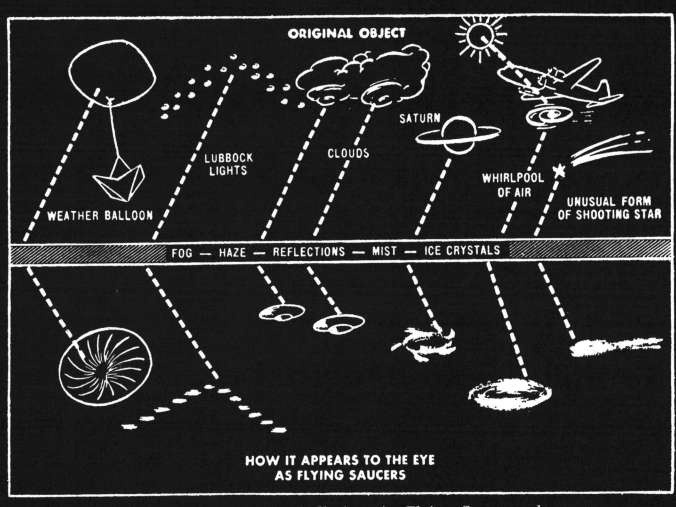

An explanation of the optical illusions in Flying Saucers phenomena.

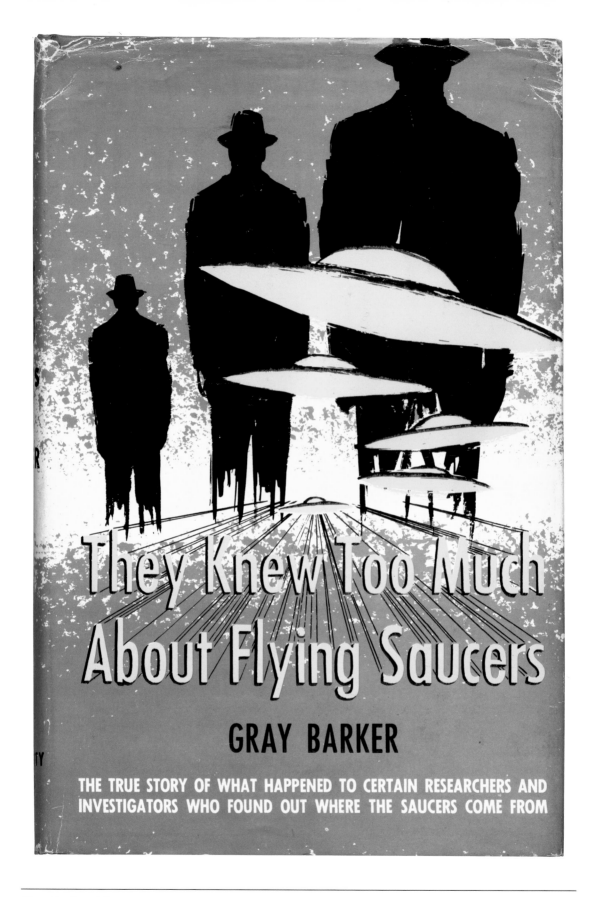

Gray Barker. *They Knew Too Much About Flying Saucers.* New York: University Books, 1956. Clothbound with dust jacket. 256 p. Dedication copy, inscribed on dedication page: "My 1st Edition / To Augie and Randy 'Dom' Smith / From Gray love ya July 56 / The Truth shall / —set you free." **Following pages: Left:** illustration from Wendelle C. Stevens and August C. Roberts. *UFO Photographs Around the World, Volume 1*, p. 146. **Right:** Front cover of *The Saucerian* no. 2, drawn by Albert K. Bender, reproduced from Gray Barker, ed. *The Strange Case of Dr. M. K. Jessup.* Clarksburg, W.V.: Saucerian Books, 1963, 1967 ptg.

GRAY BARKER AND MATTERS SAUCERIAN

●　●　●　●　●　●　●　●　●　●　●　●

West Virginia movie theater booker Gray Barker (1925–1984), a complex figure with wild talents for both hoaxing and propagandizing, published a series of books whose underlying themes (distrust of government, military conspiracies, aliens among us) and outward motifs (Men in Black, Mothman) became over the course of fifty years the aspects of Saucerology most readily refitted to today's paranormal popular culture.

He was first on the scene in 1952 to investigate a nearby saucer landing–several boys claimed to see a disc crash, and a giant alien floating over the ground toward them. (The case is known today as the Flatwoods Monster Hoax.) After selling his lively account to *Fate*, Barker started his fanzine, *The Saucerian*. He began corresponding with fellow enthusiast Albert K. Bender, who ran the first saucer investigation group (the International Flying Saucer Bureau) out of the attic of his parents' house in Connecticut. In late 1953 Bender wrote an editorial in the last issue of his own fanzine, *Space Review*, hinting of threats and concluding "*we advise those engaged in saucer work to please be very cautious.*" Barker tells of Bender's terrifying experiences and those of others in *They Knew Too Much About Flying Saucers* (1956), highlighting the importance of the men in black suits.

In 1962 Barker convinced Bender to write up his experiences for his Saucerian Press. *Flying Saucers and the Three Men* (1962) reveals the long-kept secret to be that the men in black come from secret underground polar bases, anticlimactic considering the build-up.

> There are no such things as flying saucers.
>
> The government has told you that. President Eisenhower himself stated to a saucer-conscious public that to his knowledge no one was coming here from another planet to pay us a visit.
>
> If you believe in Donald H. Menzel, President Eisenhower, and Government announcements, you need have no fear of being frightened by this story. Read it on a stormy night, or in the middle of a graveyard if you wish. Your equanimity will not be challenged.
>
> Unless you don't believe in Donald H. Menzel, President Eisenhower, and government announcements.
>
> In that case you just might be scared.
>
> — Gray Barker, *They Knew Too Much About Flying Saucers*, pp. 11–12

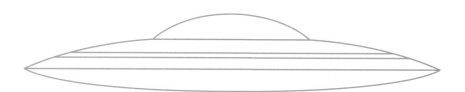

On a November evening a good movie was playing locally, and I decided to take it in. The night was damp and quite chilly; no stars were out and the sky was black as printer's ink.

About halfway through the movie I began experiencing a strange sensation. I fancied that someone had his eyes upon me, though attendance was poor and I couldn't actually spot anybody who was looking at me. But the odd feeling continued along with a prickly sensation in the back of my neck, as if the hairs were bristling up. I was most uncomfortable and began to fidget about in my seat. Suddenly I felt the presence of a person in the seat next to me, though nobody had been there previously. I had heard nobody enter and sit down.

I took a quick glance, without turning my head, and saw a man sitting there; then the eyes drew my attention. I turned my head facing him and found myself looking straight into two strange eyes, like little flashlight bulbs lighted up on a dark face. The eyes seemed to burn right into me. Before I looked away I was also struck by his clothing. There wasn't anything exactly strange about it, and it is difficult to describe what was "wrong" with it. Somehow it appeared too neat to be ordinary—that is the best way I can explain my unusual reaction to it.

I felt a spinning in my head and the movie screen blurred. I blinked my eyes several times, then closed them for a few seconds. When I opened them the man was gone; yet I had heard no movement. Then, glancing at the seat to the left of mine, I found him there, still looking at me with those eyes!

— Albert K. Bender, *Flying Saucers and the Three Men*, pp. 45–46

The SAUCERIAN

VOL. I NO. II — Published by GRAY BARKER — Clarksburg, W. VA.

NOV. 1953

35¢

REPORT ON
THE BRUSH
CREEK SAUCER

BENDER

Gray Barker, UFO Authority

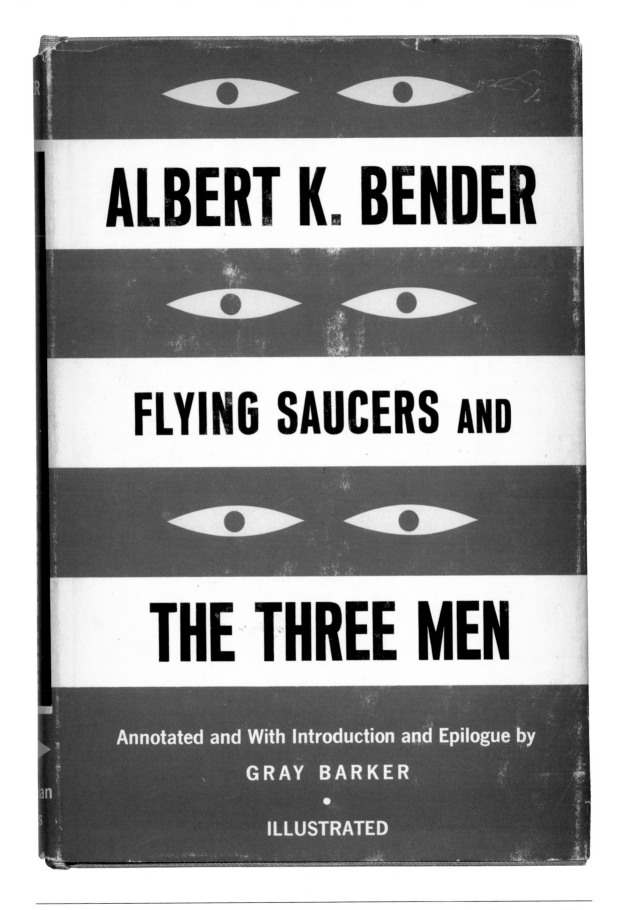

Frank E. Stranges. *Stranger at the Pentagon.* Van Nuys, CA: I.E.C., Inc., 1967. Perfect bound in wrappers. 201 p. Illustrated. **Opposite:** Photos from p. 73. **Albert K. Bender.** *Flying Saucers and the Three Men.* Clarksburg, WV: Saucerian Books, 1962. Clothbound with dust jacket, 194 p. Annotated and with introduction and epilogue by Gray Barker. **Albert K. Bender.** *Flying Saucers and the Three Men.* London: Neville Spearman, 1963. Clothbound with dust jacket, 194 p. First British edition. **Following pages:** Illustrations by Bender from pp. 107 & 121.

The author's rough sketch of one of the three men.
The eyes glowed like two flashlight bulbs.

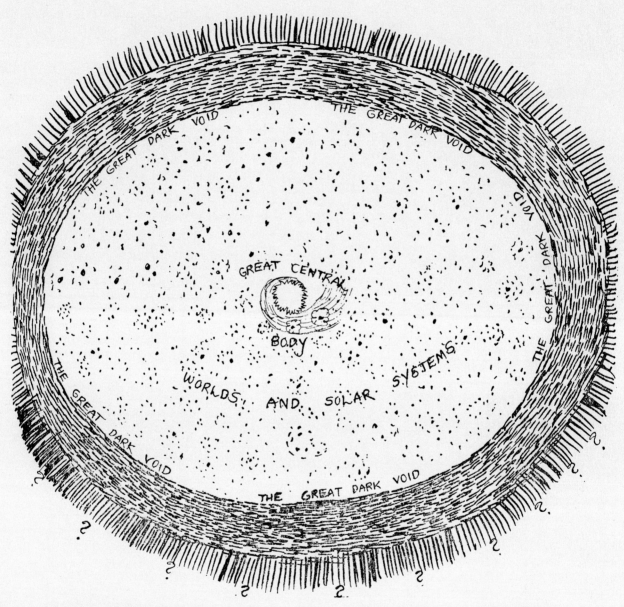

The author's sketch of the universe, with the great central body from which everything is formed and hurled into space, with its destination the great dark void. What is beyond? . . .

UFO
WARNING

By JOHN STUART

SAUCERIAN BOOKS *G. DUPLANTIER*
CLARKSBURG, W. VA.

John Stuart formed the New Zealand Flying Saucer Investigation Society in 1953 and was an early correspondent of both Barker and Bender. In *UFO Warning* (1963), he tells of meeting beautiful young Barbara Turner – real name Doreen Wilkinson, the only other member of the NZFSIS – and how his wife failed to appreciate their demanding need to investigate the saucers, most evenings. The narrative takes a very disturbing turn as a "loathsome, hideous, evil, disgusting, horrifying" being (see illustration) appears to them, making sexual advances toward Turner before vanishing; a few nights later, thirteen such beings manifest in her bedroom, and three of them rape her. In December 1954 Stuart and Turner shut down the organization, and went their separate ways.

The thing was about four or five feet away from me. It was facing me in all its vile, base hideousness. Its body resembled, vaguely, that of a human. From the waist up it was a man, and from the waist down that of a woman. Its flesh, stinkingly putrid, seemed to hang in folds. It was a grayish color. Evil exuded from the entire thing. The slack mouth was dribbling, and the horrible lips began to move, but there was no sound.

I realized with a shock that it was talking to me, using telepathy to converse. I was being warned not to proceed any further with my research. It seemed to laugh at me, and told of how others had suffered because they had attempted to solve the enigma. Like Barbara! [...]

At that point the thing seemed to waver, and grow less distinct; then it materialized again into solidity. I almost collapsed in horror and revulsion as the male and female areas of its body had suddenly changed places.

"You have been warned! Take heed! Should you fail there will be others to suffer!"

— **John Stuart,** ***UFO Warning*, pp. 79–80**

John Stuart. *UFO Warning.* Clarksburg, WV: Saucerian Books, 1963 (second printing, 1967). Perfect bound in wrappers. 82 p. Illustrated. Introduction by Gray Barker; illustrations by Gene Duplantier. **Following pages:** Illustrations by Duplantier from pp. 66 & 61.

G. DUPLANTIER

$3.95

THE STRANGE CASE

OF DR. M. K. JESSUP

Edited By Gray Barker

ILLUSTRATED

SAUCERIAN BOOKS
CLARKSBURG, W. VA.

Gray Barker, ed. *The Strange Case of Dr. M. K. Jessup.* Clarksburg, W.V.: Saucerian Books, 1963 (3rd printing, 1967). Large trade paperback, perfect bound. 79 p. Illustrated.

Morris K. Jessup (1900–1959) never completed his doctorate in astrophysics, nor did he participate in archaeological digs in the Yucatan in the 1920s, as he and others claimed on more than one occasion. He brought abiding Fortean interests to *The Case for the UFO* (1955), which sold well. One of his supposed readers, a man identifying himself as Carlos Allende, wrote two letters to Jessup telling of having seen a US Navy warship disappear from the Philadelphia Naval Yard in 1943, and the horrible things that happened to its sailors–spontaneous combustion, catatonia, disappearing from view in the midst of a bar fight. Jessup set the letters aside, at the time.

In 1956 Jessup published *UFO and the Bible*, and at his publisher's request he put together *The UFO Annual* (1956), both of which appeared within a matter of months of each other. By the time his *The Expanding Case for the UFO* (1957) appeared, he had saturated his own market; and all saucer books had finally begun to stop selling by that time, in any event.

Sometime in the midst of this–the story goes–a paperback copy of *The Case for the UFO* arrived at the Office of Naval Research in Washington, DC, where Major Darrell L. Ritter, USMC Aeronautical Project Office, ONR received it. He passed it on to Captain Sidney Sherby and Commander George W. Hoover, who asked Jessup to look at it. This appears to have possibly happened, for the Department of the Navy, in its official statement on the matter, notes "the pages of the book were interspersed with hand-written comments which alleged a knowledge of UFOs, their means of motion, the culture and ethos of the beings [Jemi, Mr. A, and Mr. B, as they referred to themselves, within the text] occupying these UFOs, described in pseudo-scientific and incoherent terms."[1]

Here is an example of a conversation between annotators [all spelling and capitalization *sic*]:

> I am Not adverse to saying that a Force-Field *Can* Make a Man to fly FOR I HAVE SEEN IT DONE & I know the cause of this flight & Am Not disturbed Paris Exhibition 1951, Scientiest from Paris Universigy Demonstrated this. AN AP PHOT WAS SENT TO U.S. SHOWING THIS ACTION.

> US NAVYS FORCE-FIELD EXPEIRMENTS 1943 OCT. PRODUCED INVISIBILITY OF CREW & SHIP, FEARSOM RESULTS. SO TERRIFYING AS TO, FORTUNATELY, HALT FURTHER RESEARCH.

On the next page, responding to Jessup's statement, "Crews have mysteriously disappeared from ships–sometimes within sight of their home port–without warning and without trace" the subtle observation:

> HEH! IF HE ONLY KNEW WHY, HE'D DY OF SHOCK.

---

1. Department of the Navy, Office of Naval Research. "Information Sheet: Philadelphia Experiment." *Naval History & Heritage Command.* Naval History & Heritage Command, September 8, 1996. Web. < http://www.history.navy.mil/faqs/faq21-2.htm >. Accessed July 2, 2014.

In its statement the Navy further notes "Jessup concluded that the writer of those comments on his book was the same person"–Carlos Allende–"who had written him about the Philadelphia Experiment."[2] [Use of that phrase would imply the official Navy statement was not prepared until the 1970s]. The story continues that this annotated copy was transcribed and published in an edition of 100 mimeographed copies by the Varo Manufacturing Company, a military supply company in Texas.

Jessup's wife left him in 1958, and he was in a serious car accident later that year. Depressed and financially overwhelmed, he was found dead in his car in 1959, an apparent suicide.

In 1963 Gray Barker published a high-drama version of Jessup's experiences, *The Strange Case of Dr. M.K. Jessup*. The two men were correspondents from 1954 until Jessup's death. They discussed money problems, and royalties, but nowhere in their surviving correspondence are found any references to Allende, or the ONR, or the so-called Varo edition published at the behest of the ONR.

No copies of the original Varo edition are known, and evidence of its existence ultimately originates in claims made by Gray Barker who–following the wider dissemination of the Allende story into public awareness in the late 60s by Ivan T. Sanderson, Brad Steiger, and others, published *The Case For the UFO: the Varo Annotated Edition* in 1973, under the Saucerian imprint, with his own introduction. Considering the frequency with which the three annotators fall back upon the time-honored phrase, "Heh!" we can only wonder.

---

2. Ibid.

George Brinsmaid displaying a fish which smashed his windshield on the streets of the nation's capital. Washington *Evening Star*, December 22, 1955. (Star Staff Photo)

M.K. Jessup, ed. *The UFO Annual.* Plate opposite p. 192.

M.K. Jessup. *The Case for the UFO: Unidentified Flying Objects.* New York: The Citadel Press, 1955. Clothbound with dust jacket. 239 p. Illustrated. Introduction by Frank Edwards. With an 8 p. pamphlet laid in: "The UFO Reporter: a Supplement to The Case for the UFO by M.K. Jessup."

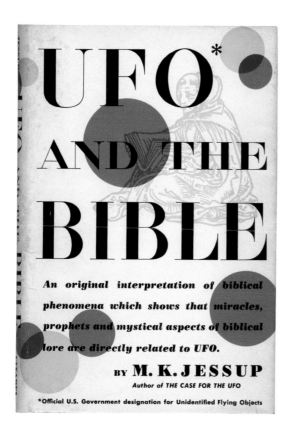

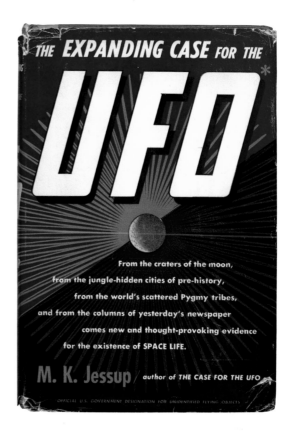

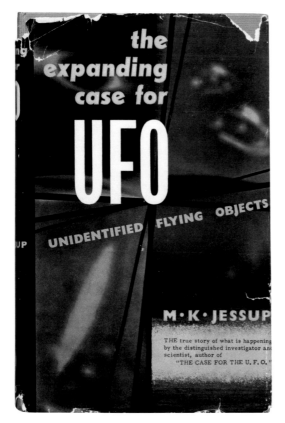

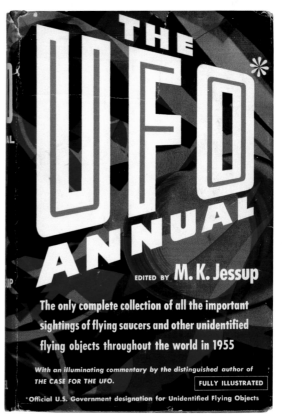

M.K. Jessup. *UFO and the Bible.* New York: Citadel Press, 1956. Clothbound with dust jacket. 126 p.
M.K. Jessup. *The Expanding Case for the UFO.* New York: The Citadel Press, 1957. Clothbound with dust jacket. 253 p. Illustrated. **M.K. Jessup.** *The Expanding Case for the UFO.* London: Arco Publications Limited, 1957. Clothbound with dust jacket. 240 p. Illustrated. First British edition. **M.K. Jessup.** *The UFO Annual.* New York: The Citadel Press, 1956. Clothbound with dust jacket. 375, 4 p. + [8] p. of plates. Illustrated. **Following pages:** Illustration from Jessup, *The Case for the UFO*, p. 107.

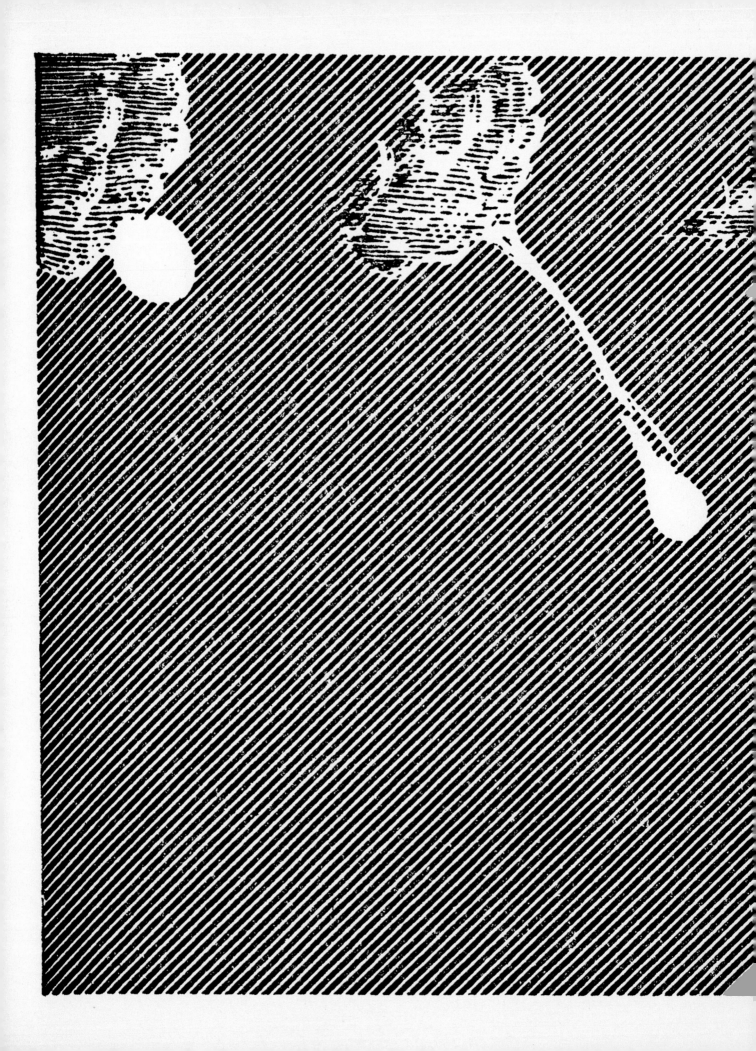

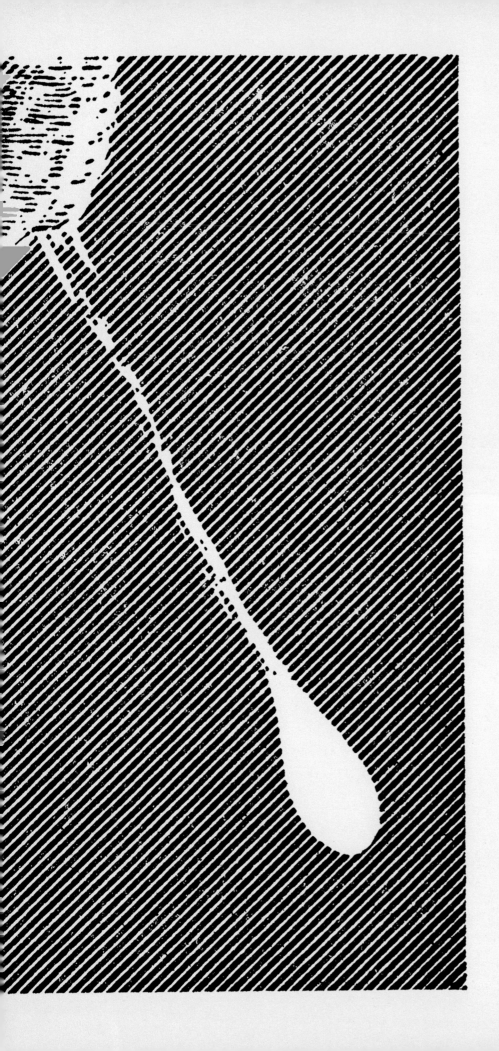

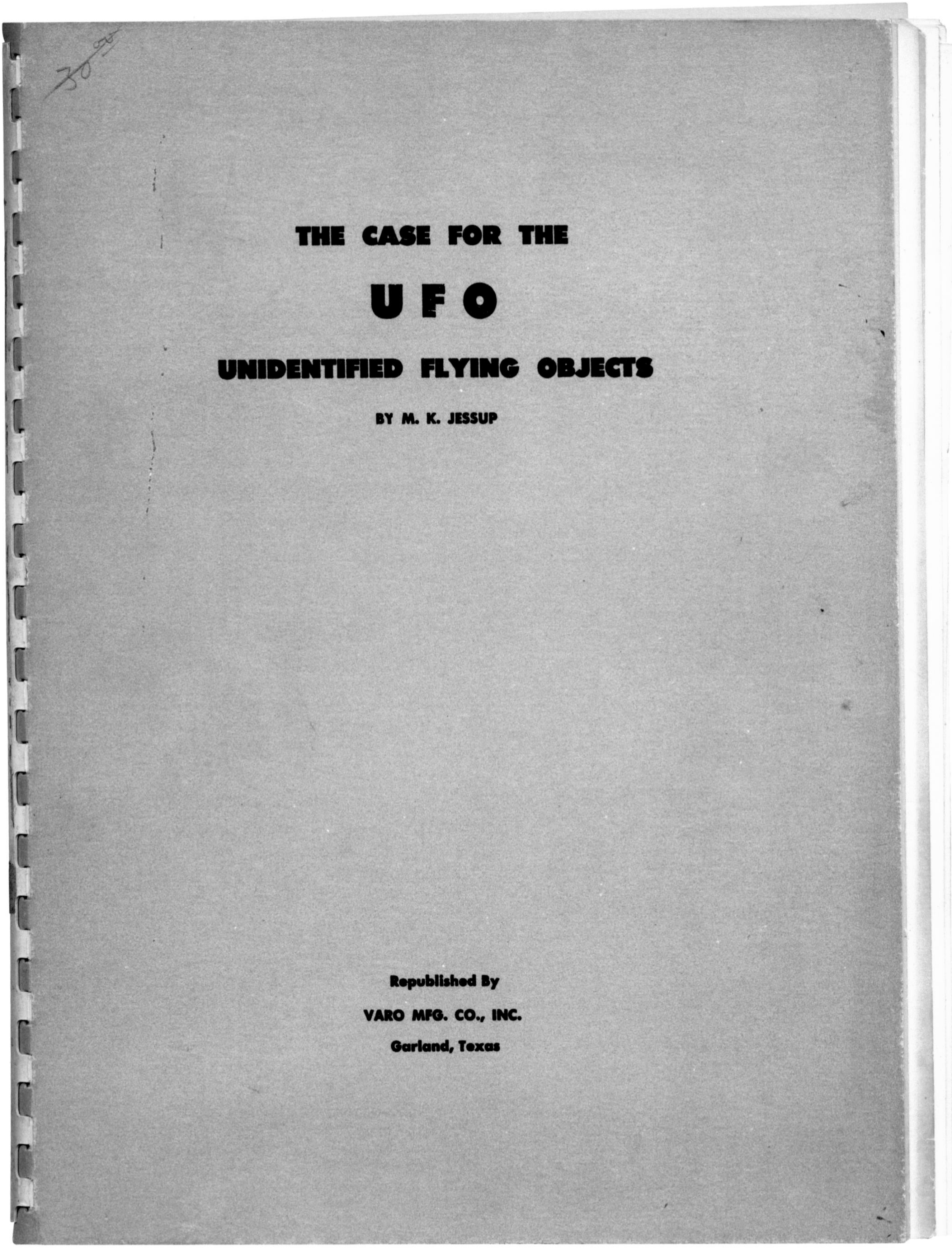

THE CASE FOR THE

U F O

UNIDENTIFIED FLYING OBJECTS

BY M. K. JESSUP

Republished By

VARO MFG. CO., INC.

Garland, Texas

M.K. Jessup. *UFO: Unidentified Flying Objects.* Clarksburg, WV: Saucerian Press, Inc., 1973. In wrappers, comb bound. vii, 189 p. "Reprinting of this edition does not imply authorization or approval by Varo, Inc." Facsimile reprint of an edition of 100 copies allegedly published by the Varo Manufacturing Co. **Opposite:** Text from p. 125.

Force Cutter, full blast. (Mr. B)

But the singular fact of these vitrified forts is that the stones are
vitrified in streaks, as if special blasts had struck or played upon them. (B)

Bdra! He's hit it, on the nose! (Underscore by A) (Mr. B)

Lightning? At any rate, once (or more) upon a time something melted,
in streaks, the stones of forts on the hills of Scotland, Ireland, Brittany
and Bohemia. Whoever, or whatever did it, they, or it, had some handy way
of getting around. Lightning has a way of hitting things prominently dis-
played on hilltops. But some of the vitrified forts are inconspicuously located and yet didn't escape; their walls, too, are vitrified in streaks. (B)
But, on hills and mountains all over the rest of the world are remains of
forts which have not been vitrified. I have in mind Sacsahuaman, on top
of the Andes at Cuzco.

ANCIENTS WARS, TOO WERE THE CAUSE, BY "F" CUTTER (Mr. B)

In this instance of forts partially vitrified, in streaks, we have one
of the most outstanding examples of selection and segregation--attributed to
intelligence. Not only do we have forts of a certain circumscribed area
picked out for attention, but we have such a high degree of concentration
and direction that only streaks in certain forts are vitrified. (B)

Boe da lograni tash na Stendic og daeli mork (Mr. B)
"Pielidismacraeli!" Stones cut with "P" at
full power of "F" cutter.

(139)

UPON REVIEW, I believe this Man MAYBE being (Mr. A)
"Iluminated" Telepathically. Somebody, L-M
or S-M is Making him write about that which
he "sees" in his head & has checked upon to
Verify. THAT somebody wants to come out of
Hiding. Not be Misunderstood, or feared but
Wants to co-exist in a Very Peaceful fashion.
OR IS PLANNING ON MAKING THE GAYORI THEIR
ALLIES, FOR WAR. IF THIS IS SO THEN ONLY THE
S-M'S WOULD WANT WAR. THEY ARE IMMATURE &
only they are SO immature as to desire War.
One planet in the Galaxy Means Nothing to
them, all they foster is "War as a Game to
alleviate their boredomish, unplayful, un-
happy existence. THE NON-PHILOSOPHISM OF
HUMAN & S-M = DESTRUCTION.

Barker was also involved in spreading initial word about the 1966–1967 sightings in and around Point Pleasant, West Virginia, notably those regarding the creature that came to be known as Mothman. Barker's *The Silver Bridge* (1970) was the first published account of the events, which involved sightings of giant red-eyed birds, even larger bird-like figures, nightly lights in the sky, the sudden appearance throughout the area of both men in black and peculiar individuals claiming otherworldly origin–the most notable encounter of these being Woodrow Derenberger's in 1966 with a man who rode in a vehicle resembling a "kerosene lamp chimney," wore a glistening green outfit, and called himself Indrid Cold. Events came to a sudden end with the collapse of the Silver Bridge into the Ohio River on December 15, 1967, killing 46. In *The Silver Bridge* Barker provides the narrative that would years later be expanded upon by John Keel in the far better known *The Mothman Prophecies* (1975).

I had just fallen asleep, when, I swear, a voice with a very odd accent boomed into my room, saying, *"What do you want?"* I sat up wide awake, turned on my light, and looked at my dog to see if he was aware of anything. He was still asleep.

I lit a cigarette, and was thinking it must have been a dream, or that I had too much to drink, or that my imagination was playing tricks on me. After a few more drags on the cigarette I became convinced of this.

Then, booming through the entire upstairs floor, the voice, still with the odd accent, said: *"Have you called us? What do you want?"* My first reaction was that I should say, "Shh, you'll wake up the whole house!" Again I looked at the dog which was still asleep; then (forgetting the reason I had wanted to see or talk to them) I replied:

"WHAT ELSE HAVE YOU GOT BESIDES FLYING SAUCERS?"

I waited in vain for an answer, and deeply regretted my crude remark. Finally, I got up and wrote this down on paper, but it was really unnecessary. I should have made some notes on the *accent*, for the next morning I remembered everything else except the odd accent.

— **Gray Barker, *The Silver Bridge*, p. 120**

Gray Barker. *The Silver Bridge.* Clarksburg, WV: Saucerian Books, 1970. Clothbound with dust jacket. 151 p. Inscribed on front free endpaper: "To / Gladys Fulsom / with all best / wishes / Gray Barker / July 24 1970." The colophon states that the book was printed in Amherst, Wisconsin: Barker used Ray Palmer's printing company, Tomorrow Rivers, for several of his publications.

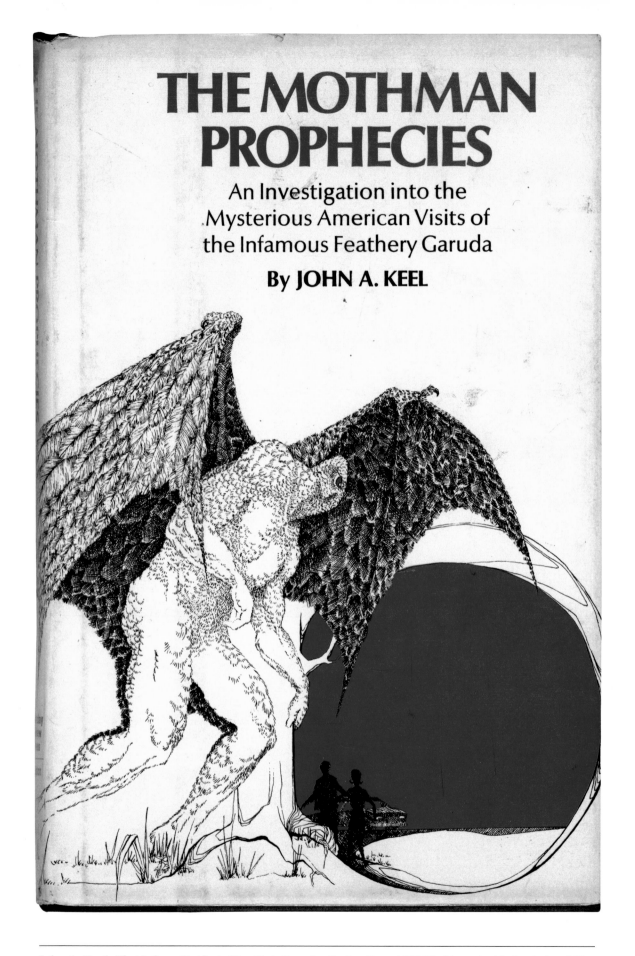

THE MOTHMAN PROPHECIES

An Investigation into the
Mysterious American Visits of
the Infamous Feathery Garuda

By JOHN A. KEEL

John A. Keel. *The Mothman Prophecies.* New York: Saturday Review Press, 1975. Clothbound with dust jacket, 269 p.

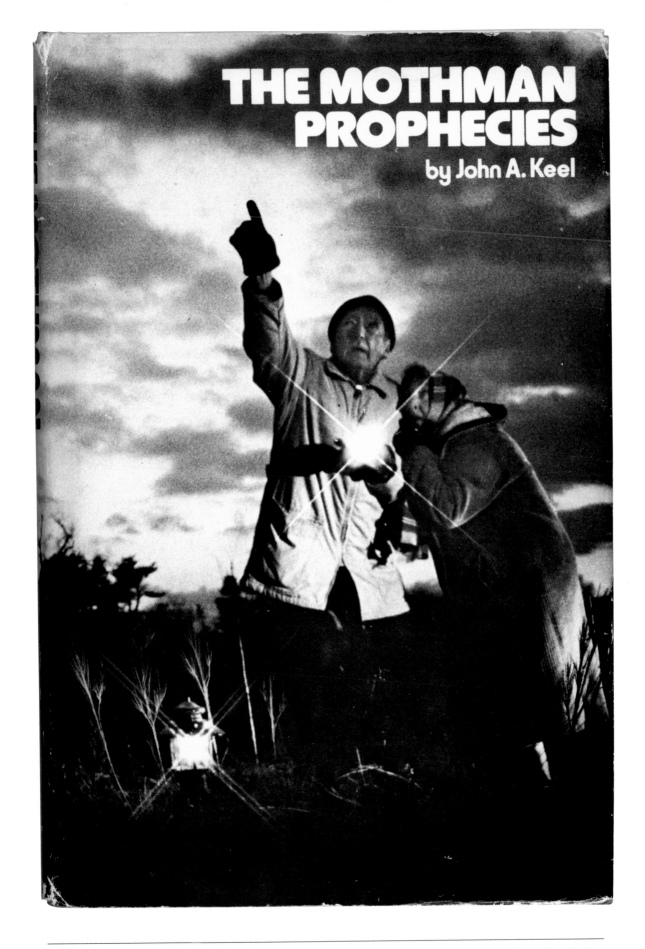

John A. Keel. *The Mothman Prophecies.* New York: Saturday Review Press, 1975. Paper-covered boards with dust jacket, 238 p. Book club edition.

HOW TO CONTACT
SPACE PEOPLE

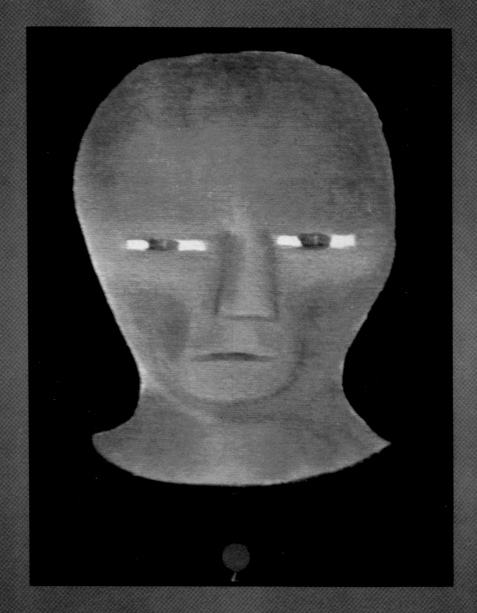

By TED OWENS

ILLUSTRATED

SAUCERIAN PUBLICATION/CLARKSBURG, W. VA.

MEANWHILE, IN THE OFF WORLD COLONIES

● ● ● ● ● ● ● ● ● ● ● ●

In the wake of science's official denial of UFO existence, new theories by the saucerload, bound neither by rules of physics nor of logic, began to appear as ufology became more of a specialist's game.

MENSA member Ted Owens (1920–1987) claimed to have conversations with Space Intelligences (SIs), energy beings sometimes appearing in the guise of insects. Also claiming to possess the power of psychokinesis, and calling himself "PK Man," he bent metal spoons with mental energy, claiming as well to control the weather and earthquakes. He explained that repeated head injuries he'd suffered earlier in life had been caused by the SIs so that he could both perform these wonders and, later in life, communicate with them. He explains how others may get in touch with them in *How to Contact Space People* (1969), another Saucerian Press classic.

> Now, for your amusement, and because you've been so good to listen to me for so long, I will let you in on something. I am calling fleets of UFOs here, to Philadelphia, from everywhere. Trouble is I do not know what they can do to prove to these people here that I'm for real. But I will think of something. I believe they are here already, because I sent for them this afternoon. With all that power, whatever kind it is, that they have—and it seems to be miraculous, judging from what they've accomplished this past year—they should do something startling. Am trying to convey the idea to them of coming right down over the city and hovering. But they give me the idea back that we might have some kind of rays like they have, or whatever it is they have, and hurt them or something, so that they are reticent to do this. So I am trying to tell them we haven't any such thing, and that it's safe for them to appear.
>
> **— Ted Owens, *How To Contact Space People*, pp. 23–24**

Ted Owens. *How to Contact Space People.* Clarksburg, WV: Saucerian Publications, 1969. Perfect bound in wrappers. 96 p. Illustrated. With coupon for an "SI Disc" and Saucerian Publications order form laid in.

"What, me worry?"

In 1968 the body of a horse in Colorado named Snippy was presented as the first animal thought to be deliberately mutilated by aliens (or, possibly, someone posing as aliens). During the next few years a wave of similar killings, though more often of cattle, transpired throughout North America. Although each individual death was readily attributable to natural causes, interest in Cattle Mutilation *qua* Cattle Mutilation took off like that in Chupacabra, twenty years later. The first book entirely on the subject, *Mystery Stalks the Prairies* (1976), was followed by other local and often self-published accounts such as Gene Duplantier's *The Night Mutilators* (1979) and Project Stigma's *The Choppers–and the Choppers* (1991). In the early 80s Bantam Books published *Mute Evidence*, a thoroughly researched debunking of the entire subject; to which, naturally, no attention was paid.

In most cases of animal deaths of this sort, no tracks or evidence of a struggle are ever found. Phantom helicopters piloted by fanatics are suggested as the means of getting to and from the scenes of the crime without leaving evidence of a visit. Is some kind of covering material used to avoid showing tracks or footprints? And it has happened in all kinds of weather conditions too. Who has the money to finance such ventures?

— Gene Duplantier,
The Night Mutilators, p. 7

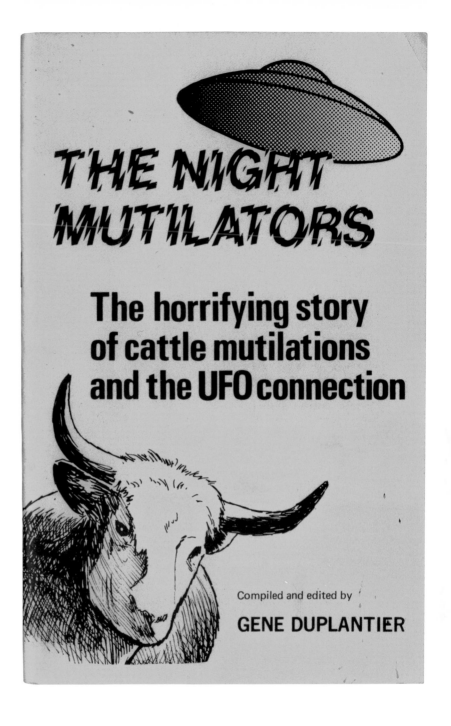

THE NIGHT MUTILATORS

The horrifying story of cattle mutilations and the UFO connection

Compiled and edited by
GENE DUPLANTIER

Gene Duplantier, ed. *The Night Mutilators: The horrifying story of cattle mutilations and the UFO connection.* North York, Ontario, Canada: SS&S Publications, 1979. Pamphlet in wrappers, saddle stapled. 60 p. Illustrated. **Opposite:** Illustration from p. 43.

THE CATTLE MUTILATIONS MYSTERY—SOLVED!

FINALLY, THE INCREDIBLE
TRUTH BEHIND THE WAVE OF DEATH
THAT SHOCKED THE NATION.

Daniel Kagan and Ian Summers

Daniel Kagan & Ian Summers. *Mute Evidence.* Toronto and New York: Bantam Books, 1984. Mass-market paperback. xix, 504 p. **Opposite:** Illustration from Duplantier, *The Night Mutilators*, p. 29.

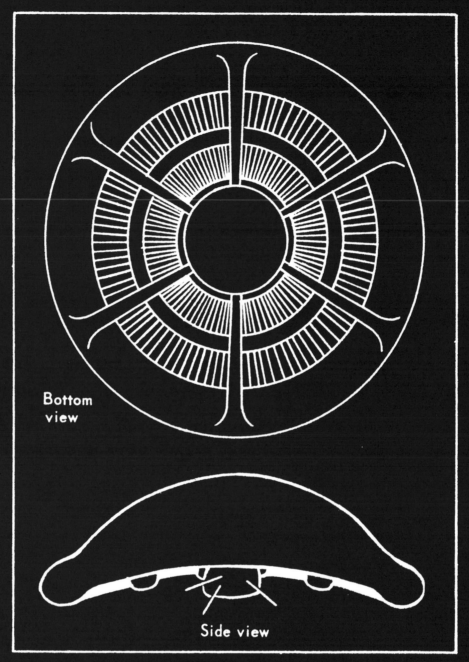

Bottom view

Side view

About an hour or so later, he let his horse graze by
the stream to regain its composure. Heading back to
the pasture not far from where he spotted the UFO, his
horse started to stiffen up again as if she heard or
smelled something. The man's imagination started working again thinking there was another one of those things
around. Then he spotted a horse lying down on its side
and rode over and looked at the horse whose hair was
singed and burnt off. The horse was dead. Its eyes
were still open and rigor mortis had not yet set in.
There was no way of knowing whether the horse had died
in terror. For a few days afterwards, his horse's ears
were quite sensitive and he had a hard time trying to

THE CHOPPERS — AND THE CHOPPERS

MYSTERY HELICOPTERS AND ANIMAL MUTILATIONS

REVISED EDITION

Thomas R. Adams. *The Choppers–and the Choppers: Mystery Helicopters and Animal Mutilations.* Paris, TX: Project Stigma, 1991. Photocopied pamphlet in wrappers, saddle stapled. 39 p. Illustrated. Revised ed.

Roberta Donovan and Keith Wolverton. *Mystery Stalks the Prairie.* Raynesford, MT: T.H.A.R. Institute, 1976. Perfect bound in wrappers. 108 p. + [16] p. of plates. Illustrated. Photographs by Ken Anderson. Signed by the authors.

John Keel (1930–2009) authored one of the last great travel narratives (*Jadoo*, 1957) before becoming interested in Forteana in general, and cryptozoology and flying saucers in particular. He eventually conceived a wide-ranging theory that proposes, in essence, that whatever the operative intelligences behind the paranormal may be they have a perverse, and dangerous, sense of humor. For a while in 1969 he published his own zine, *Anomaly*, afterward writing his classic works *Strange Creatures from Beyond Time and Space, UFOs: Operation Trojan Horse* (little noted at the time, but in successive decades proving to be a major influence on the development of ufological thought) and the afore-mentioned *The Mothman Prophecies* (1975). In later life seeming more cynical about the matters at hand (if in no way less believing), he lived to see the events of Point Pleasant make it to the big screen–if only to hear the film's character "Leek" provide the immortal line re: Mothman, "It's what the UKRAINIANS called him." It's not.

Already the erstwhile members of the Fortean Society, fans and follow-ers of the late Charles Fort, were warming up in the bullpen. They had the answer even before they knew what all the questions were. You see, it worked out this way: In 1945, we dropped our atom bombs on Japan. The bombs sent a blast of energy into space, where it was detected by the sensitive instruments of superintelligent beings on oth-er worlds. Said beings were terribly concerned that poor, bumbling man had discovered the secrets of atomic energy. So an expedition to the earth was formed to investigate. However, some superintelligent navigator made a slight error. Instead of leading his spaceships down to troubled Japan, he missed by a wide margin and ended up in Scandinavia instead. Sorry about that.

— **John A. Keel, *UFOs: Operation Trojan Horse*, pp. 137–138**

Buried within the context of all the contactees' messages there are clues to an even more complex threat. A direct threat to us. Each contactee has been able to pass on a small fragment of the real truth. The endless descriptions of peaceful far-off worlds and shining cities of glass are only subterfuges. Before I can extend this further, I must present you with some of the other evidence. You must be aware of all the pieces in the puzzle before they can fall into place and make sense. Already you can under-stand why so many people have been in total confusion for so long. This whole mystery has been designed to keep us confused and skeptical.

Somebody somewhere is having a good laugh at our expense.

— **John A. Keel, *UFOs: Operation Trojan Horse*, p. 214**

John A. Keel. *UFOs: Operation Trojan Horse.* New York: G.P. Putnam's Sons, 1970. Clothbound with dust jacket. 320 p.

ANOMALY

No. 1 May 1969

<u>FLYING SAUCERS.</u> This is the first and last time you will
see those two words in this publication. We hope to est-
ablish <u>ANOMALY</u> as an irregular newsletter devoted entirely to the statistical and scientific analysis of all the
many neglected ecological, parapsychological and psychia-
tric aspects surrounding the study of aerial anomalies
(AA). We are primarily concerned with collecting and
correlating all known AA events in a systematic manner
so that we may eventually produce a valid body of
statistical and corroborated evidence. This project will
in no way compete with existing organizations. It is not
a "club". No membership cards will ever be issued. We
do not seek or desire publicity. Our only purpose is to
assemble the available facts and present them to the
press and the public in a logical, unbiased manner. We
have no ax to grind, no "cause" to prove.

A large proportion of all the available UFO literature
is based upon hearsay and speculation, and many of the
real and important problems have been suppressed at the
source by the witnesses themselves, or have been ignored
by superficial investigations which were concentrated on
obtaining descriptions of the objects rather than studying all of the events and factors surrounding the sightings. A massive body of sighting data has now been published but has gone uncorrelated. The practice of con-
centrating on the objects alone has produced a very low
yield of "hard" facts. The failure of this method-or
lack of method- demands that we develop and utilize a
new system for collecting and analysing the data.

This issue presents some concrete suggestions for investigating the phenomena and it explains briefly some of
those findings which appear to contradict the popular
speculations. We hope that you will begin to apply these
methods in your own immediate area and that you will
participate in our study by submitting new reports (and

MAY O 1 1969

No. 2 Sept. 1969

Plus assorted supplementary material.

editor: john a. keel

John A. Keel, ed. *Anomaly, no. 1, May 1969.* New York: Specialized Research, 1969. Pamphlet in wrappers, side stapled. 16 p. **John A. Keel, ed.** *Anomaly, no. 2, Sept, 1969.* New York: Anomaly, 1969. Pamphlet in wrappers, side stapled. pp. [19]–38.

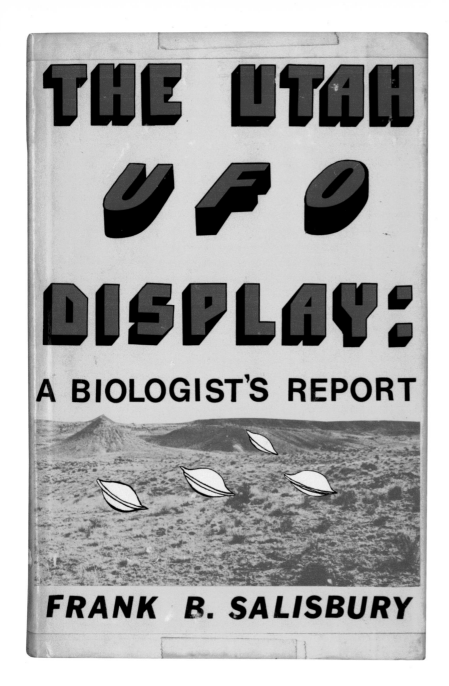

The number of perceived sightings grew throughout the 1970s, the Condon Report notwithstanding, often being recorded in regional compilations such as Dr. Frank Salisbury's *The Utah UFO Display* (1976), one of numerous titles focusing upon sightings within a single state. Dr. Salisbury studies sightings in Utah's Uinta Basin, bringing a semblance of actual scientific reason to his examinations before comparing saucer sightings to religious visions.

Frank B. Salisbury. *The Utah UFO Display: A Biologist's Report.* Old Greenwich, CT: The Devin-Adair Company, 1974. Clothbound with dust jacket. xxiv, 286 p. + [16] p. of plates. Illustrated. **Opposite:** Back of jacket.

THE WAY THEY LOOKED:

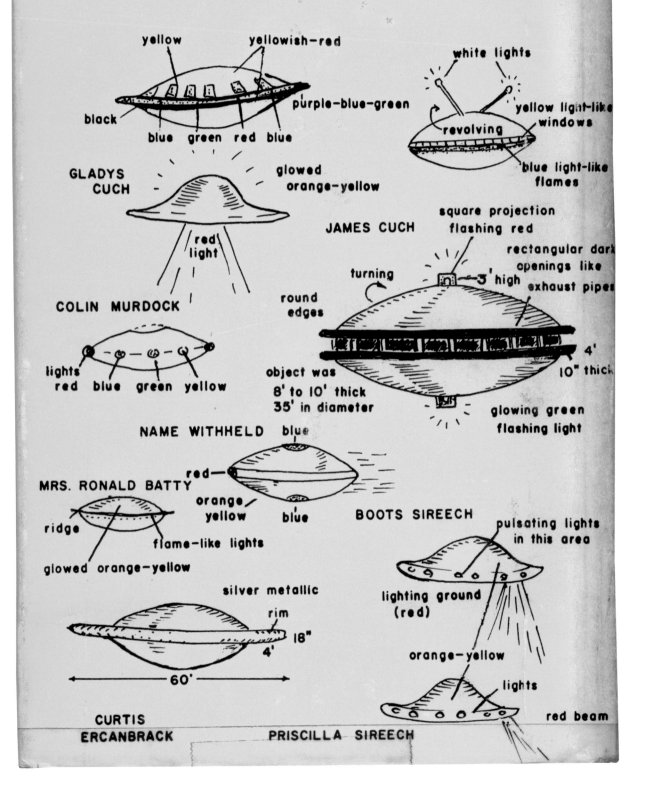

BRENT D. YOUNG

CARLOS REED

yellow
yellowish-red
white lights
purple-blue-green
yellow light-like windows
revolving
black
blue light-like flames
blue green red blue

GLADYS CUCH

glowed orange-yellow

square projection flashing red

JAMES CUCH

rectangular dark openings like exhaust pipes

turning

3' high

round edges

red light

COLIN MURDOCK

lights
red blue green yellow

object was
8' to 10' thick
35' in diameter

4'

10" thick

glowing green flashing light

NAME WITHHELD   blue

red

orange/ yellow   blue

MRS. RONALD BATTY

ridge

BOOTS SIREECH

pulsating lights in this area

flame-like lights

glowed orange-yellow

lighting ground (red)

silver metallic

rim

18"

4'

orange-yellow

lights

60'

red beam

CURTIS ERCANBRACK

PRISCILLA SIREECH

Don't Look Up! The Real Story Behind the Virginia UFO Sightings (1988) by Danny Gordon and Paul Dellinger is another regional work, this one focusing on sightings in the area of mid-seventies Wytheville, Virginia, later covered on a segment of TV's *Unsolved Mysteries*.

Danny B. Gordon and Paul Dellinger. *Don't Look Up!: The Real Story Behind the Virginia UFO Sightings.* Madison, NC: Empire Publishing, Inc., 1988. Perfect bound in wrappers. 208 p. Illustrated. Large print edition. **Opposite:** Illustrations from pp. 150, 158, 169. **Following page:** Illustrations from p. 96, 139.

clear casing   bright as stars

UFO craft seen by an anonymous UFO spotter.

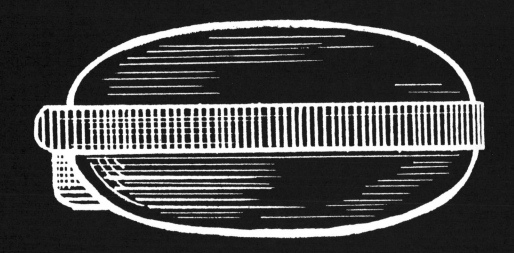

One might suggest that the Scout Ship-Type Craft resembles a hamburger.

The craft depicted in this drawing reflected the moonlight, and its shape was clearly visible. The color of the craft, appeared dark; all of its lights were white and constant. At arm's length, the craft seemed to be approximately 8 to 12 inches in length.

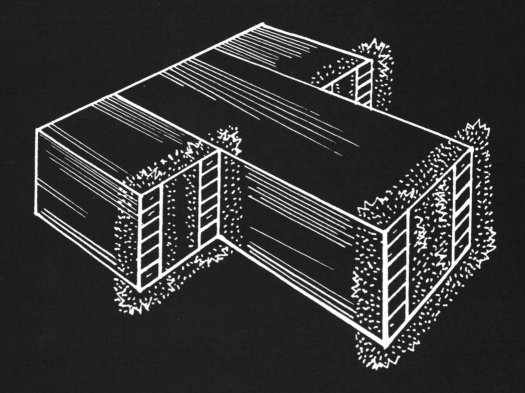

The Rectangular-Type Craft (T-ship) has been spotted
by various persons in the Wytheville area.

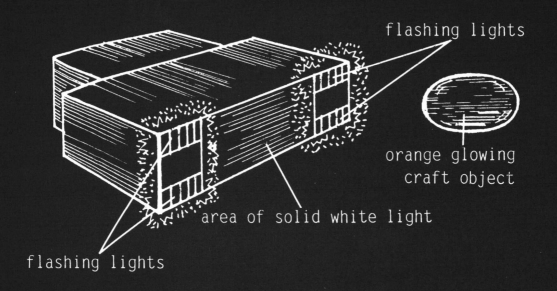

flashing lights

orange glowing
craft object

area of solid white light

flashing lights

Here is a drawing of a rectangular craft.

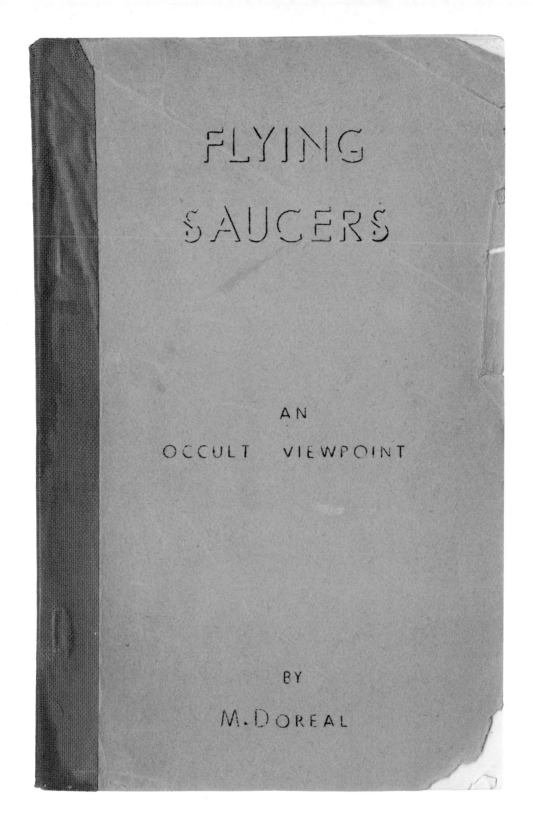

M. Doreal's *Flying Saucers: An Occult Viewpoint*, mimeographed on cheap paper, staple bound, appearing under the auspices of the Brotherhood of the White Temple, was published sometime in the mid-1950s. The Brotherhood, still in operation and readily reachable at www.bwtemple.org, was founded by Dr. Doreal in 1930. His most famous work is his interpretation and translation of *The Emerald Tablets of Thoth the Atlantean*, which should indicate the worth of this particular text.

M. Doreal. *Flying Saucers: An Occult Viewpoint.* Sedalia, CO: Brotherhood of the White Temple, [ca. 1951–1963]. Mimeographed pamphlet in wrappers, side-stapled with tape strip. 45 p.

Allen Michael, author of *UFO-ETI World Master Plan* (1977) was a later exemplar of the post-contactee contact movement. His organization, The Universal Industrial Church of the New World Comforter, can be found at galacticmessenger.com. Michael, whom the site notes "was an incarnate spiritual master from Galactica, a God-conscious soul dedicated to serving humanity" died in 2010, age 93.

You have never before seen so many New Age organizations popping up—people telling the truth. These are those who have come out of this old dying world order and are transcending on the New Age energies being beamed into this planet's aura. ["]Only the people who open up to total sharing ways and means of all things will be standing in the lot at the end of these days["] (Daniel 12:1-13). You'd better believe it!

The question is: "How do we make liberty, justice and equality real?" The answer is: We begin to build a *Uni Economic System* of true sharing, in which all things flow from the vine of life (the world vineyard of Nature's God) to bless all people directly. Then the *US citizens of Israel* will truly "become a blessing to all the families of the earth," as foretold in Gen. 12:1-3.

The Uni Godhead's hand of destiny, thru the six men and women of the ETI Adamen (Freemasonry) team, saw to it that the Bill of Rights did get into the US Constitution—but it came after the men of the Adamen had compromised on letting private banks operate in the new US, believing that later they could be properly legislated. As we see, they never could, and now the US economy is stagnated and coming to its end, and the people are being led into another big war to see who is going to "rule the world." Ha! Very funny! No group of earth people are going to rule the planet. It is being returned to the Universal Order of planets.

— **Allen Michael, *UFO-ETI World Master Plan*, pp. 154–155**

Allen Michael. *UFO-ETI World Master Plan: Channelings from the Everlasting Gospel.* [N.p.]: One World Family Starmast Publications, 1977. Mass-market paperback. 159 p.

$1.95 One World Family
STARMAST PUBLICATIONS

UFO-ETI WORLD MASTER PLAN

by Allen Michael

ETI — Extra Territorial Intelligence — tells

How to transform this planetary civilization, in as little as 90 days, into its New Order for the Ages.

How to offset calamity—the upcoming "last war for the world"—before it comes.

How US World Citizens fulfill prophecy becoming "a blessing to all families of the earth."

Arthur Shuttlewood (1920–1996) worked as a reporter in the UK for many years, but when he decided UFOs were evidence of extraterrestrial beings, he announced that he could no longer be an independent observer. In the years following he became one of the leading, and evidently more charismatic figures in British ufology. In all of his books, beginning with *The Warminster Mystery* and continuing in later volumes such as *UFO Prophecy* (1978), it is clear that Shuttlewood's journalistic skills were especially adept when it came to transforming the mundane into the apocalyptic.

UFO IN THE DOCK

Men drew all day, with eager speed,
A new ship to produce ;
A blueprint soon drawn up, complete
For all the craftsmen's use.

Down in the yard things were prepared,
The work was due to start ;
The workers gathered round the berth
To lay the first small part.

For many months they slaved away,
Till all was nearly done ;
The tension rose as final staves
Were duly placed thereon.

Then something seemed to go awry—
And all, bewildered, cowered ;
For on the berth, for all to see,
A flying saucer towered !

— **Arthur Shuttlewood,** *UFO Prophecy*, **p. 230**

Arthur Shuttlewood. *UFO Prophecy.* New York: Global Communications, 1978. Perfect bound in wrappers. 266 p. Illustrated.

UFO PROPHECY

ARTHUR SHUTTLEWOOD

Among Brad Steiger's many, many paranormal titles was *UFO Missionaries Extraordinary* (1975), the story of a man and woman going by the names Bo and Peep, who showed up in Oregon calling themselves "The Two," and claiming to be the only extraterrestrial emissaries on earth. They explained to sell-out audiences that their goal was to provide humanity with a more ascetic day to day regimen: a quiet life, a few possessions, celibacy; and then they went away for awhile. The second act of The Two (real names Marshall Applewhite and Bonnie Nettles) took place years later in the San Diego suburbs when they reappeared, the leaders of a group called Heaven's Gate, some of whose male members castrated themselves so as not to be tempted away from the celibate life. On March 19, 1997, all 39 members–including Bo and Peep–committed suicide in order that their souls might rendezvous with a spaceship, in advance of the approaching Hale-Bopp Comet.

Brad Steiger's *The Flying Saucers Are Hostile* (1967), like so many of this author's books on the subject, is a choice example of many of the saucer titles appearing during these years: exploitative, anecdotal, fast-moving, seemingly written in less than a day.

> If the aliens have really come to share such an easy existence with us, why have they left men with no evidence of contact, other than radiation sickness, first-degree burns, or, at best, memory lapses? Why have the UFOs burned children with direct-ray focus, destroyed remote villages, and attacked aircraft and land vehicles?

> — **Brad Steiger, *The Flying Saucers are Hostile*, p. 10**

> There is little doubt that the Russians are quite impressed by the mysterious discs which have demonstrated that they are quite capable of 'shutting off' missile stations, snatching planes and parachutists out of the sky, outmaneuvering both interceptor jets and missiles, and obliterating sections of factories after activating alarm systems to avoid needless loss of life.

> — **Brad Steiger, *The Flying Saucers are Hostile*, p. 84**

Brad Steiger and Joan Whritenour. *Flying Saucers are Hostile.* New York and London: Award Books/Tandem Books, 1967. Mass-market paperback. 160 p. + [16] p. of plates. Illustrated.

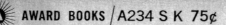 AWARD BOOKS / A234 S K 75¢

BECAUSE OF THE TERRIFYING IMPLICATIONS OF ITS FULLY DOCUMENTED EVIDENCE, THIS MAY WELL BE THE MOST STARTLING BOOK YOU WILL EVER READ!

FLYING SAUCERS ARE HOSTILE

UFO Atrocities from strange disappearances to bizarre deaths

By Brad Steiger, author of STRANGERS FROM THE SKIES
and Joan Whritenour, editor of SAUCER SCOOP

**WITH 16 PAGES OF PHOTOGRAPHS
AND THE INDEPENDENT LABORATORY
ANALYSES OF UFO RESIDUES!**

Basil Tyson's *UFOs: Satanic Terror* is a fairly typical example of the contemporary Christian approach, warned of being led astray by misguided scientists, yet paying no heed to the likes of Bo and Peep.

We have also urged the reader to avoid all contact with occult practices and manifestations of spiritism. This applies to everyone, but is especially relevant to those with a special awareness of the unseen world. Parapsychology comes into the realm of areas to be avoided.

Whether the reader has had personal experience with UFOs and the unseen world or not, the answer for all who are concerned for their spiritual safety and welfare is straightforward. First, it is to make certain that they are rightly related to God through His Son, Jesus Christ.

The Bible teaches, "For God so loved the world, that he gave his only begotten Son, that whosoever believeth in him should not perish, but have everlasting life" (John 3:16).

To "believe in Jesus Christ" means to face the fact that "all have sinned, and come short of the glory of God" (Romans 3:23), and so call upon Him for total forgiveness for all our sins. It also means to turn from our sins to follow Him from that point on. This is the path of safety and assurance. I pray you'll take it.

The answer for those with special awareness or experience in these realms is also straightforward.

It is to "abide in Christ." When this is our blessed condition we have nothing to fear, and Satan himself is powerless against us.

— Basil Tyson, *UFOs: Satanic Terror*, pp. 113–114

Basil Tyson. *UFOs: Satanic Terror.* Beaverlodge, Alberta, Canada: Horizon House Publishers, 1977. Mass-market paperback. 122 p.

HORIZON BOOKS $1.95

Foreword by Dr. Clifford Wilson, author of CRASH GO THE CHARIOTS

UFOs
Satanic Terror

BASIL TYSON

A PICTORIAL TOUR
OF UNARIUS

Unarius (Universal Articulate Interdimensional Understanding of Science) was founded as a nonprofit organization in Los Angeles in 1954 by Ernest Norman (1904–1971). The group's stated purpose: to advance awareness of the inter-dimensional science of life as based upon principles of fourth-dimensional physics. Unarius published over 100 books transcribing channeled conversations with space brothers and other-dimensional beings, as well as overviews such as *A Pictorial Tour of Unarius*. Ernest met his wife Ruth Norman (1900–1993) in Glendale, where she attended his lectures. After his death she served as the organization's public face, appearing in her finery once on "Late Night with David Letterman." Her death, and more predictably the failure of a space fleet predicted to materialize on earth in 2001 to actually land, negatively affected the operation.

The Universal Hierarchy. *A Pictorial Tour of Unarius.* El Cajon, CA: Unarius Educational Foundation, 1982. Perfect bound in wrappers. 166 p. Illustrated. **Opposite:** "Third Dimensional Spacecraft as They Will Land on Earth," p. 3.

The Universal Hierarchy. *A Pictorial Tour of Unarius.* **Opposite top:** "Model for New Age Cities," p. 19. **Opposite bottom:** p. 45. **Above:** p. 43.

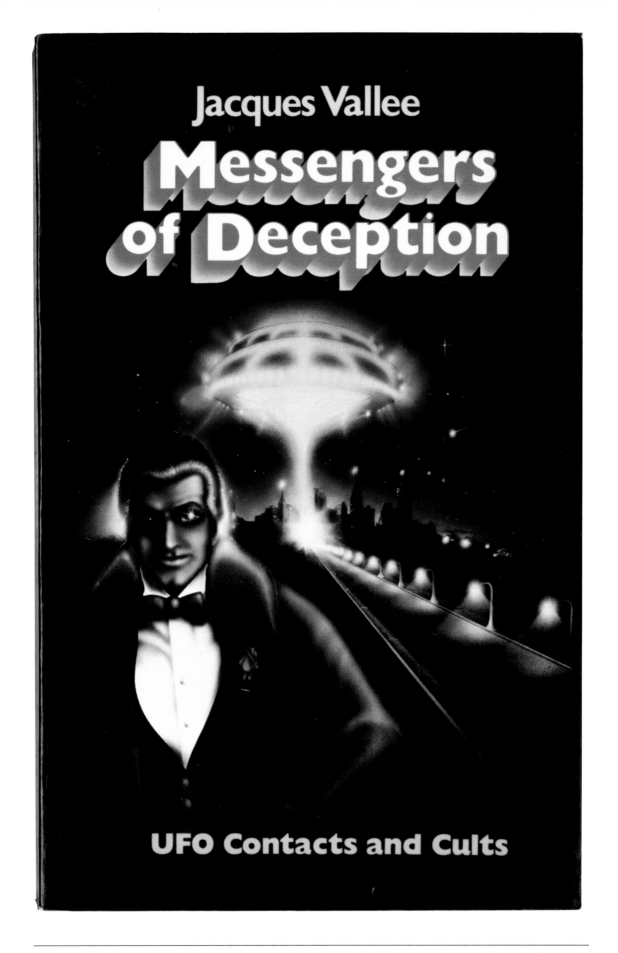

Jacques Vallee. *Messengers of Deception: UFO Contacts and Cults.* Berkeley, CA: And/Or Press, 1979. Perfect bound in wrappers. viii, 243 p. Illustrated. **Opposite:** Photo from p. 29.

Figure 1.1. Pascagoula, Mississippi: Shipyard worker Charlie Hickson describes the October night in 1973 when he says, an unidentified flying object landed in the old Schaupeter shipyard. Hickson claims three "things" picked him and young Calvin Parker up, and carried them aboard the craft, where they were closely examined.

Jacques Vallee, author of the bestselling *Anatomy of A Phenomenon* (1962) and real-life model for Francois Truffaut's character in *Close Encounters of the Third Kind*, developed over time his own version of Keel's theory—that paranormal forces were to some degree toying with us, though to a much more subtle point in the mind of Vallee, as he writes in *Messengers of Deception* (1979).

Let me summarize my conclusions thus far. UFOs are real. They are an application of psychotronic technology; that is, they are physical devices used to affect human consciousness. They may not be from outer space; they may, in fact, be terrestrial-based manipulating devices. Their purpose may be to achieve social changes on this planet. Their methods are those of deception: systematic manipulation of witnesses and contactees; covert use of various sects and cults; control of the channels through which the alleged 'space messages' can make an impact on the public.

— **Jacques Vallee, *Messengers of Deception*, p. 21**

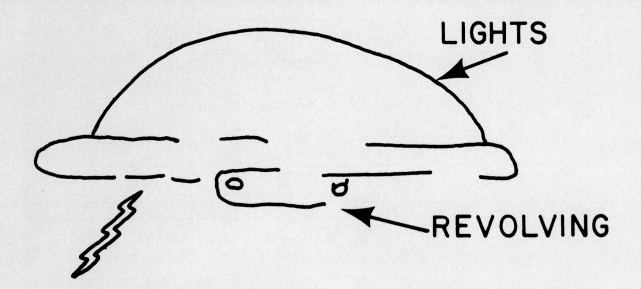

LIGHTS

REVOLVING

LIGHTNING BOLT
COMING OUT OF
BOTTOM OF ONE

FROM HEAVEN TO EARTH

One of the more notable characters still at work after multiple decades on the UFO scene, Timothy Green Beckley continues to republish the more delightful Saucerian Press titles as well as new titles that may well have given even Gray Barker pause. *The UFO Silencers* (1990, new editions continually in print) is his take on the Men in Black situation, as coherent and understated as one would expect from the author of *Kahuna Power*, *The American Indian UFO Starseed Connection*, and the recently released *Evil Empire of the ETs and the Ultra Terrestrials*.

Timothy Green Beckley. *The UFO Silencers.* New Brunswick, NJ: Inner Light Publications, 1990. Perfect bound in wrappers. 160 p. Illustrated. Foreword by John A. Keel. **Opposite:** Illustrations from Vallee, *Messengers of Deception*, pp. 167 & 117. **Following pages:** Illustrations by Carol Ann Rodriguez from Beckley, *The UFO Silencers*, pp. 88 & 67.

Dr. Hopkins was visited by zombie-like individual who made a coin vanish from inside the MD's clenched fist and warned him in "no uncertain terms" to drop his investigation into a UFO abduction case he was studying. (Art by Carol A. Rodriguez)

Psychic impressionist Carol Ann Rodriguez depicts typical rendering of MIB based upon hundreds of testimonials.

In contrast to Beckley, UK researchers Andy Roberts and David Clarke, in their *Phantoms of the Sky* (1990) in the great British tradition bring logic, sensibility, and a preference for hard evidence to their study of the situation, to no seeming avail.

David Clarke and Andy Roberts. *Phantoms of the Sky: UFOs–A Modern Myth?* London: Robert Hale, 1990. Clothbound with dust jacket. 204 p. + [8] p. of plates. Illustrated. **Opposite:** Photos from plate [3].

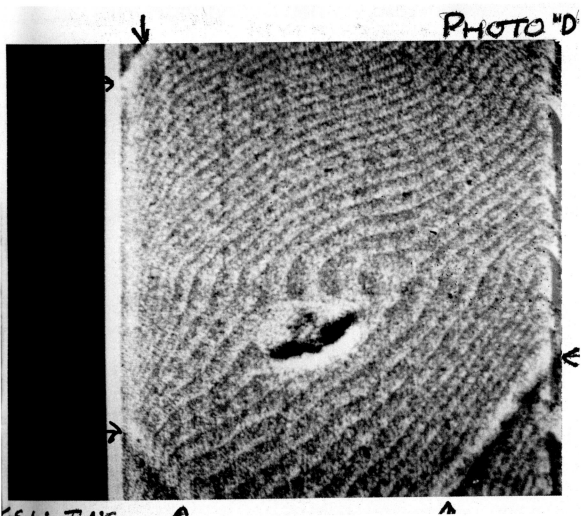

PHOTO "D"

Top: One of the series of four UFO photographs taken by fisherman Peter Beard from his home in Barnsley, South Yorkshire on the morning of 5 August 1987 (see Chapter 5). **Bottom:** One of the computer enhancements of the Beard photographs carried out by Ground Saucer Watch of Phoenix, Arizona, showing evidence of a possible double negative — another UFO bites the dust?

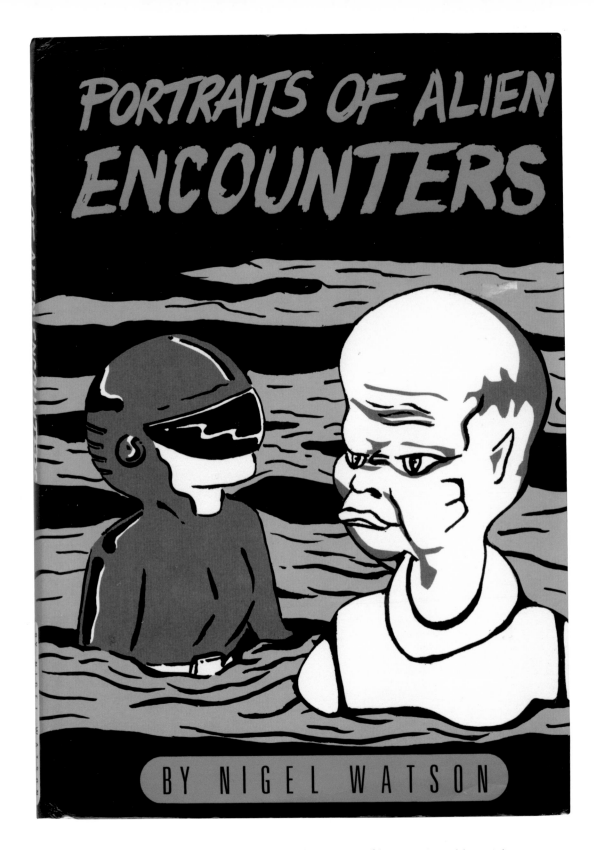

Nigel Watson's *Portraits of Alien Encounters* (1990) consists of his very sensible articles on saucers written for the journal *Magonia*. They are, however, fated never to be read so long as the book's dust jacket is seen first.

Nigel Watson. *Portraits of Alien Encounters.* London. Valis Books, 1990. Leatherbound with dust jacket. 189 p. Illustrated. Signed by the author on the title page. **Opposite:** Illustration from p. 72. **Following pages:** Illustration from p. 109.

*Spaceman seen
by Darren Sunderland in 1976*

ARONIEL

MICHAEL

Norman Harrison had psychic communications from these three entities

URIEL

Valiant Thor

Frank E. Stranges. *Stranger at the Pentagon.* Van Nuys, CA: I.E.C., Inc., 1967. Perfect bound in wrappers. 201 p. Illustrated. **Above:** Photograph from p. vi. **Opposite:** Illustration from Wendelle C. Stevens and August C. Roberts. *UFO Photographs Around the World*, Volume 1, p. 80.

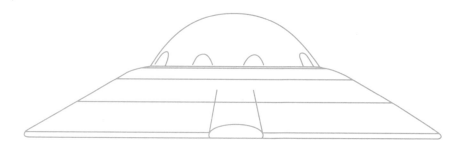

INTRODUCTION

My Name is Valiant Thor. I am a native of the planet you call Venus. It is not too unlike your Earth, in fact, we still enjoy the air-conditioned atmosphere that Earth had before the great flood.

I am on a special mission to this planet. We are over seventy in number and there are certain Earth friends working with us. In order to protect them, their names, etc., have been changed.

I have also related several incidents directly involving UFOs or Flying Saucers (as you call them). Those involved in each case have also been renamed to protect them against unscrupulous individuals who delight in making life miserable for innocent victims of circumstances.

The United Nations delegates were stunned to the point of sheer anger, mixed with fear. But, go ahead . . . . . read on. Your personal reaction will be interesting for us to record.

The following pages will reveal much . . . at least to those who are capable of discerning knowledge, wisdom and above all, understanding.

To these friends I say God bless you — to all others, God help you.

Valiant

— Frank E. Stranges, *Stranger at the Pentagon*, p. v

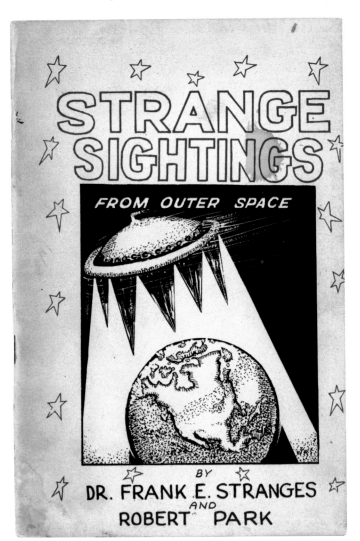

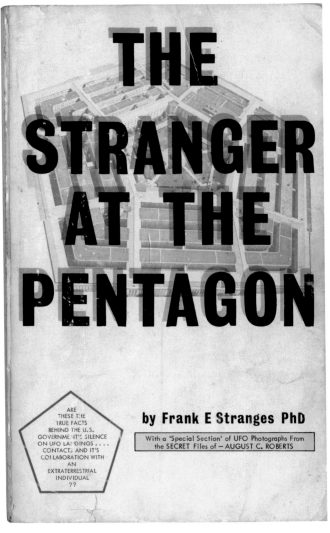

Frank E. Stranges and Robert L. Park. *Strange Sightings.* Venice, CA: Truth Publications, 1964. Pamphlet in wrappers, saddle stapled. 50 p. Illustrated. "Adapted from the motion picture, 'Strange Sightings', outline written by Robert L. Park." Prospectus for a film later completed with the title *Phenomenon 7.7.* **Frank E. Stranges.** *Stranger at the Pentagon.* Van Nuys, CA: I.E.C., Inc., 1967. Perfect bound in wrappers. 201 p. Illustrated.

There has never been a shortage of contactees, and enablers of contactees. A particularly notable representative during the 1960s was The Reverend Dr. Frank E. Stranges (1927–2008), who wrote of the blessings of Jesus, and of his pal Venusian Captain Valiant Thor with equal grace. *Strange Sightings From Outer Space* (1964) gives some indication of Dr. Stranges' constant willingness to believe what he is told, but not until *Stranger At the Pentagon* (1967) does Captain Thor fully present himself. Stranges speaks of their first meeting at the Pentagon, following the meeting to discuss peace among planets Thor had had the day before with President Kennedy and the Joint Chiefs of Staff. "The soft texture of his skin" surprised the good reverend. That same year, perhaps in hope of confusing those intending to join NICAP, he founded the National Investigations Committee on UFOs (NICUFO).

Finally the door burst open and I was ordered to follow six armed guards into what appeared to be an elevator. It sank rapidly to the bottom-most level. Maximum security was in full force.

We then transferred to an underground train which sped us toward the capitol building.

The reception committee at the other end was quite excited. Six persons, plus an additional six armed guards and three secret servicemen escorted me into the office of the President of the United States.

As we walked in I noted a worried look on the face of the President. The secret servicemen were nervous and uneasy. The President rose from behind his desk as we all walked toward him. I raised my hand to shake his—suddenly the three secret servicemen drew their revolvers and pointed them at me before my hand touch that of the President; he nervously nodded to them and they slowly lowered their guns.

Standing in front of his desk he said, "Of course, you know we have both suspended all rules of protocol. I have a good feeling toward you. Please, sir, what is your name?" I replied, "Valiant." "And, where do you come from?" "I come from the planet your Bible calls the morning and the evening star." "Venus?" "Yes, sir." "Can you prove this?" he asked; I replied, "What do you constitute as proof?" He quickly retorted, "I don't know."

— **Frank Stranges, *Stranger at the Pentagon*, pp. 19–20**

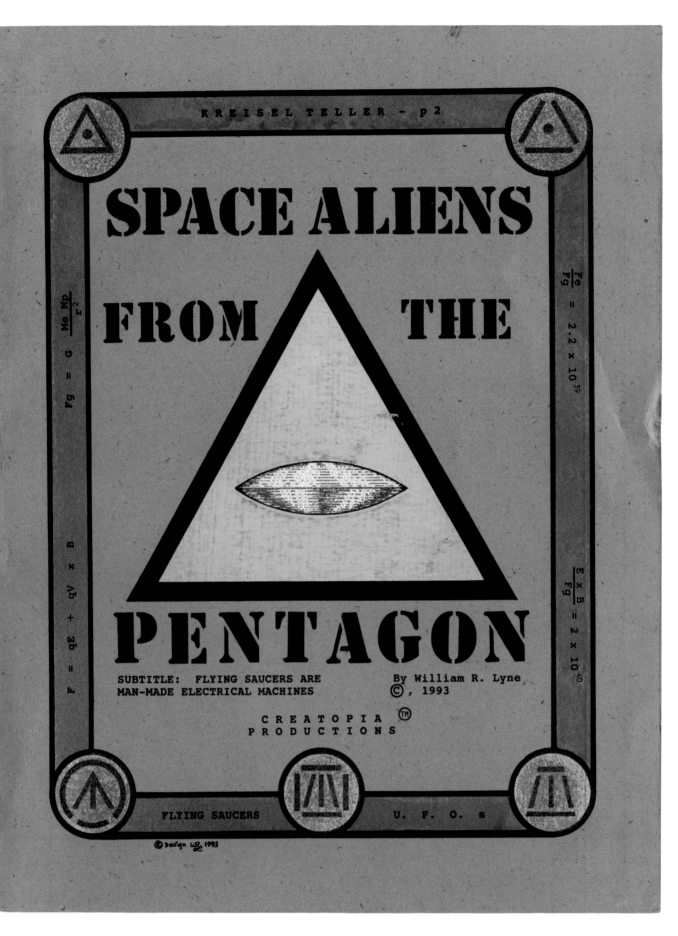

SPACE ALIENS FROM THE PENTAGON

$$Fg = G \frac{Me\, Mp}{r^2}$$

$$F = qE + qV \times B$$

$$\frac{Fe}{Fg} = 2.2 \times 10^{39}$$

$$\frac{E \times B}{Fg} = 2 \times 10^{40}$$

SUBTITLE: FLYING SAUCERS ARE
MAN-MADE ELECTRICAL MACHINES

By William R. Lyne
©, 1993

C R E A T O P I A ™
P R O D U C T I O N S

FLYING SAUCERS

U. F. O. s

© Design WRL 1993

As theories grew ever more convoluted, new titles became ever more representative of smaller demographics. William R. Lyne's *Space Aliens From the Pentagon* (1993) is an excellent example. Herein Mr. Lyne notes that Nikola Tesla invented the flying saucer in 1900 and that the US government stole it from the noted, eccentric inventor (with Edison's assistance, no doubt) so that the Nazis could further develop it at Los Alamos under the direction of Wernher von Braun and Dr. Robert Goddard, in conjunction with plans of the Trilaterial Commission, and the Illuminati. Also: Mr. and Mrs. Hitler were invited by LBJ to visit "Hemisfair," the World's Fair in San Antonio, Texas, in 1967. The author is cognizant this is not common knowledge.

I know that by publishing this book, there will be those who are poised to label me as "insane," led by the government and Trilateralist toadies. They may produce copies of court orders (invoking "privilege," as a means of avoiding civil liability), in order to "show" that I have no credibility. You should interpret those orders as I have, as injuries sustained in battle, for speaking truth to a liar judiciary. Bear in mind that those orders have been created and planted in advance, for that very purpose.

— **William R. Lyne**, *Space Aliens From the Pentagon*, **p. iii**

And finally, I am proud to be the one to reveal the fact that flying saucer technology is man-made, long known, and long suppressed by the government and Trilateralists, through a multi-layered hoax, involving a sham "national security" cover, under which a mystical, religious hoax is being used to brainwash the people. This is all to protect the corporate-state energy cartels from this technology. Public awareness of this will eventually liberate us all from energy slavery, according to the wishes of the inventor, and consistent with the U.S. Constitutional mandate to grant patents to inventors for the advancement of science and for the good of us all, without compromise.

So there you have it.

— **William R. Lyne**, *Space Aliens From the Pentagon*, **pp. 46–47**

William R. Lyne. *Space Aliens From the Pentagon: Subtitle: Flying Saucers are Man-Made Electrical Machines.* Lamy, NM: Creatopia Productions, 1993. Perfect bound in wrappers. 244 p. Illustrated. **Following pages:** Illustrations and text from pp. 220 & 76.

SPACE ALIENS FROM THE PENTAGON

1.

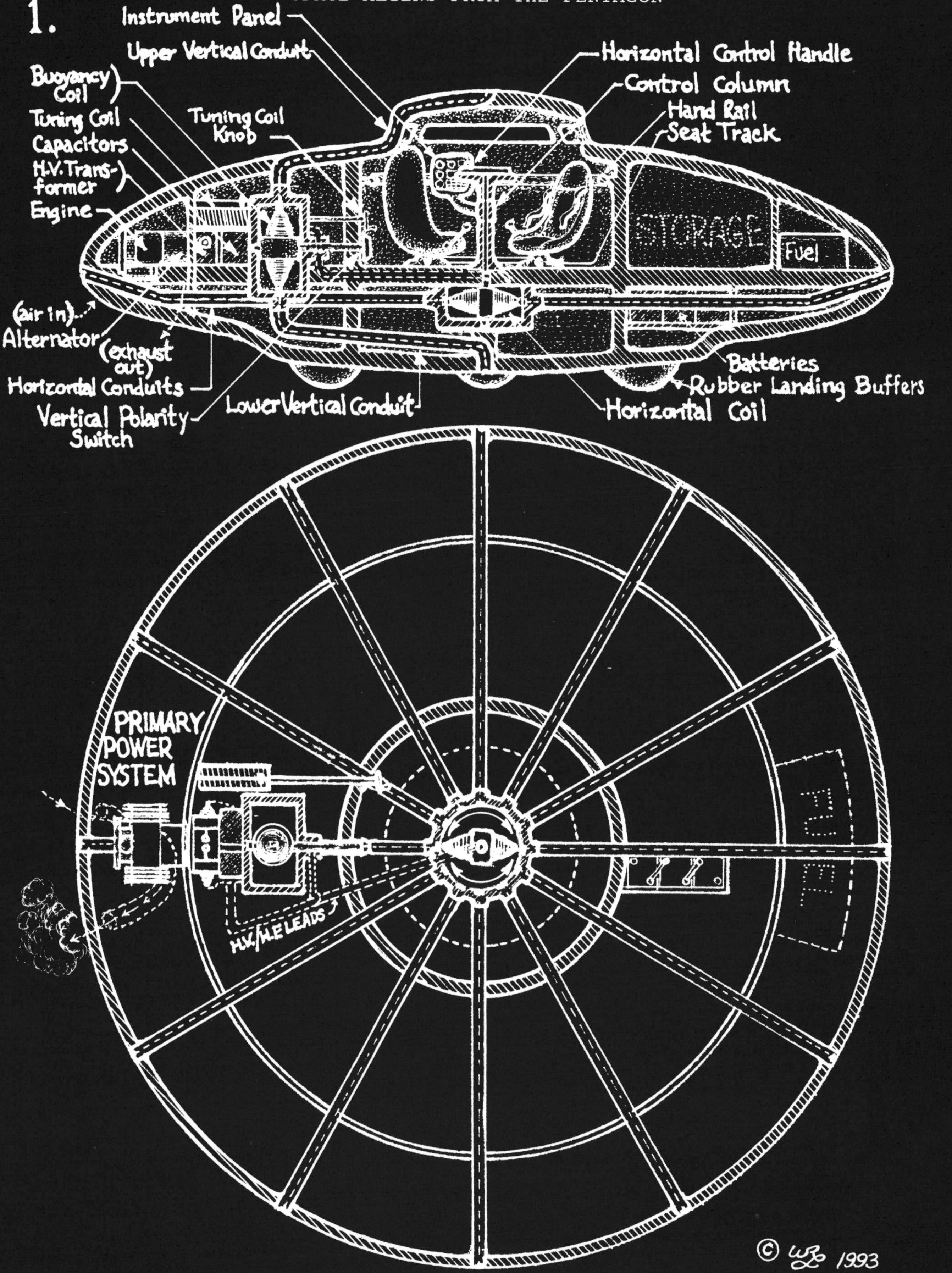

Instrument Panel
Upper Vertical Conduit
Buoyancy Coil
Tuning Coil
Capacitors
H.V. Transformer
Engine
Tuning Coil Knob
Horizontal Control Handle
Control Column
Hand Rail
Seat Track

STORAGE

Fuel

(air in)
Alternator
(exhaust out)
Horizontal Conduits
Vertical Polarity Switch
Lower Vertical Conduit
Horizontal Coil
Batteries
Rubber Landing Buffers

PRIMARY POWER SYSTEM

H.V./H.E. LEADS

© wℛℓ 1993

device used to control saucers, of the earliest types. The one I bought was from one of the saucers brought to New Mexico in the late 40s or early 50s, from Germany. The type of saucer it went on was probably of a design which preceded the type which I saw, and corresponded to the type seen by my mother in 1950. Those types were as follows:

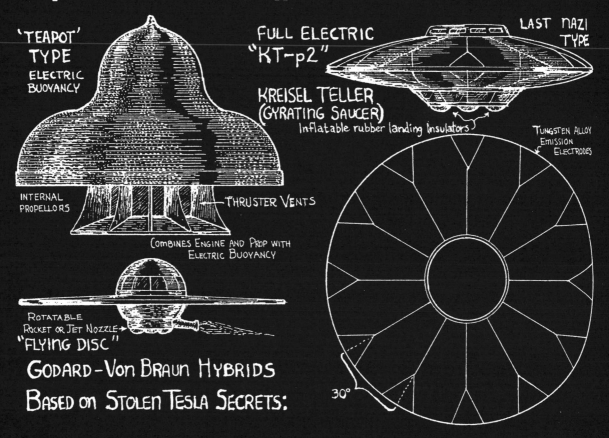

'TEAPOT' TYPE
ELECTRIC BUOYANCY

INTERNAL PROPELLORS

THRUSTER VENTS

COMBINES ENGINE AND PROP WITH ELECTRIC BUOYANCY

FULL ELECTRIC "KT-p2"

KREISEL TELLER (GYRATING SAUCER)
Inflatable rubber landing insulators

LAST NAZI TYPE

TUNGSTEN ALLOY EMISSION ELECTRODES

ROTATABLE ROCKET OR JET NOZZLE
"FLYING DISC"

GODARD-VON BRAUN HYBRIDS
BASED ON STOLEN TESLA SECRETS:

30°

While in Ohio, in 1960, I knew a girl named Gertrude Thum, whose father, Hitler's personal valet, was released by the Russians later that year. Thum was not even mentioned by other historians. On his release by the Russians, the press was not allowed to interview Thum, and he was immediately spirited away by American intelligence personnel. Only later, in the presence of intelligence personnel, was he allowed to speak to the press from a prepared statement.

The Berlin "Fuehrerbunker", completely designed by Hitler, had an 'unfinished' tower opening to the sky at its top, with a landing pad, directly accessible by private staircase from the hallway just outside Hitler's apartment in the lowest level of the bunker. The couple were rescued around sunrise, April 29th, 1945, by flying saucer test pilot Hanna Reitsch, and flight expert and navigator Hans Ulrich Rudel, who had made many flights to "Feuerland". The Russians never entered the bunker until over two full days later, just before midnight, April 2, 1945.

U.F.Os
AND THEIR
MISSION
IMPOSSIBLE

DR. CLIFFORD WILSON
AUTHOR OF "THE SEARCH"
AND "CRASH GO THE CHARIOTS!"

Dr. Clifford Wilson, best known for his anti-ancient astronauts book *Crash Go the Chariots*, later wrote *U.F.Os and Their Mission Impossible* (1975), employing a heady mixture of religious fundamentalism and CSIOP-level skepticism in his approach to the problem.

Clifford Wilson. *U.F.Os and Their Mission Impossible.* Burnt Hills, NY: Word of Truth Productions, Inc., 1974. Perfect bound in wrappers. 243 p.

The inexplicably worldwide success of Erich von Däniken's *Chariots of the Gods* in 1971 resulted in dozens of ever-more haphazardly researched books on "ancient astronauts" being published in the years after. *Mankind–Child of the Stars* (1974) by Max Flindt and Otto Binder, is one of the liveliest, doubtless for the skills Binder, who'd written many of the original scripts for *Captain Marvel* comics, brought to the project.

We sincerely feel we have dramatic evidence—very nearly proof—that will hopefully make a never-to-be-forgotten impact on the mind of the reader. An impact that will even affect scientific opinion, eventually.

— **Max Flindt and Otto Binder,**
Mankind—Child of the Stars, **p. 13**

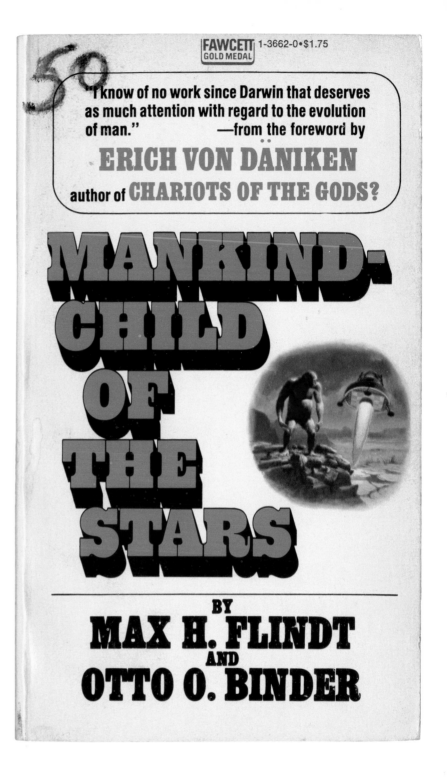

Max H. Flindt and Otto O. Binder. *Mankind–Child of the Stars.* Greenwich, CT: Fawcett Publications, 1974. Mass-market paperback. 272 p. A Fawcett Gold Medal Book. Forward by Erich von Däniken.

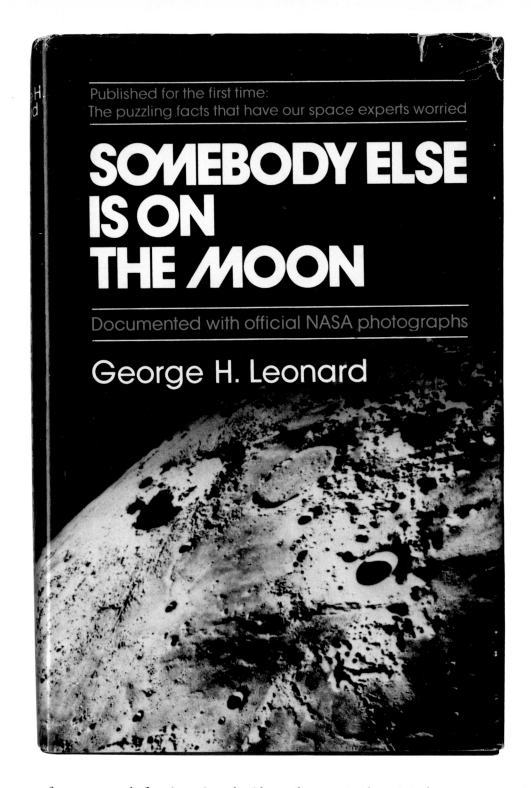

Aspects of space never before investigated with much verve in the original saucer era received greater attention during the 1970s. Not long after the initial moon landings, books such as *We Discovered Alien Bases on the Moon* (1981), *Somebody Else is on the Moon* (1976), and *Our Mysterious Spaceship Moon* (1975) began to appear, asking questions that heretofore had not come to mind. Could the moon be hollow? Could it be an alien construction? Might aliens be living there now? Possibly. Possibly.

George H. Leonard. *Somebody Else is on the Moon.* New York: David McKay Company, Inc., 1976. Clothbound with dust jacket. xix, 232 p. + [32] p. of plates. Illustrated. According to James E. Oberg's *UFOs & Outer Space Mysteries*, George later recanted his claims in this book. **Opposite:** Illustrations from pp. 107 (top) & 49 (bottom).

Top: It is clearly an octagon, and appears to be a covering, with long polelike objects sticking out from under the edges. **Bottom:** ...toward the camera a few miles from the crater lip is a Latin cross four miles long and raised off of the ground half a mile. It is in a rectangle. The Latin (or Roman) cross near Kepler looks like this.

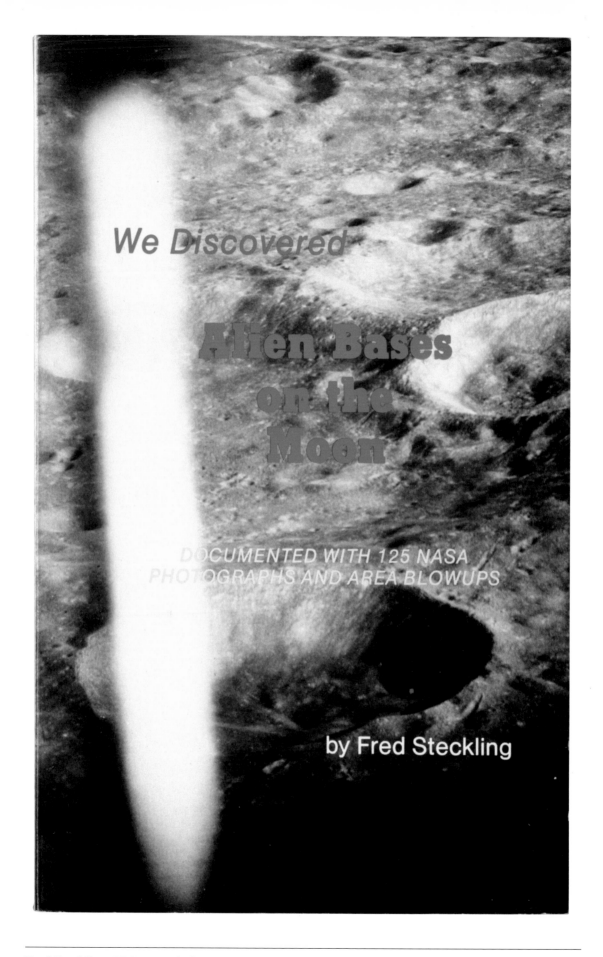

Within the image: *We Discovered Alien Bases on the Moon* / DOCUMENTED WITH 125 NASA PHOTOGRAPHS AND AREA BLOWUPS / by Fred Steckling

Fred Steckling. *We Discovered Alien Bases on the Moon.* Vista, CA: Fred Steckling, 1990. Perfect bound in wrappers. 191 p. Illustrated. 5th edition, 1990; originally published 1981.

Now the crucial missing link in the chain of evidence of *Chariots of the Gods?*

Complete with startling official NASA revelations that the moon may be a spaceship from other worlds!

OUR MYSTERIOUS SPACESHIP MOON

by DON WILSON

Don Wilson. *Our Mysterious Spaceship Moon.* New York: Dell Publishing Co., Inc., 1975. Mass-market paperback. 172 p.

raël
THE MESSAGE
Given To Me By
EXTRA-TERRESTRIALS

AOM

They Took Me To Their Planet

ARE THESE PANCAKES FROM OUTER SPACE? WHO CAN SAY?

● ● ● ● ● ● ● ● ● ● ● ●

During the last twenty years or so those still believing in UFOs have split into smaller groups, each with particular areas of interest. While the days of little gray men hustling thousands off annually to employ anal probes with gusto have faded, many more sub-cultural manifestations of the UFO world and related phenomena have gained greater popularity in successive decades: do people live inside the moon, have the CIA/NSA/FBI etc. been co-opted by the aliens (or are in fact aliens themselves), whether Bigfoot might be a pal of "space critters," whether Nazis colonized the moon while no one was looking, and so forth. In Saucerdom, there are ultimately no limits to what you want to believe; as Criswell himself said in *Plan 9 From Outer Space*, "Can you prove it didn't happen?"

In the founding document of Raëlism, *The Message Given To Me By Extra-Terrestials* (post-1973) former race car driver Claude Vorilhon (a/k/a Raël) explains that the Elohim, or extraterrestrials, created people; that on earth, Elohim are perceived as angels, gods, saucer people or the like; and that as recipient and prophet of their final message–"world peace is good"–Raël personifies the Elohim on earth. Within Raël's immediate circle is the Order of Angels, a group of young Raëlian women sworn to protect his life at any costs, and who are allowed to sleep with prophets, or the Elohim. Raëlism's symbol, a swastika embedded within a Star of David, was once in common use, but no longer. The Raëlians are perhaps best known for having falsely claimed to have cloned a baby girl in 2002.

> The financing of this realisation will be possible, thanks to the help you will obtain from those who believe in you, and therefore, in us, who will be wise and intelligent. They will be rewarded when we come. Keep a record therefore of those who contribute financially to this realisation, however modest their contribution, for the edification or upkeep of the residence, and throughout the world in each nation take a responsible person who will spread the truth, and permit people to unite themselves in spreading it.

> — Claude Vorilhon ("Raël"), *The Message Given To Me By Extra-Terrestrials*, p. 117

Claude Vorilhon ("Raël"). *The Message Given To Me By Extra-Terrestrials: They Took Me To Their Planet.* Tokyo: AOM Corporation, 1986. Mass-market paperback with dust jacket. 295 p. Illustrated. Second English edition; originally published: Montreal: Fondation Pour l'Accueil des Elohim, 1978. Translation of *Le livre qui dit la vérité* and *Les extra-terrestres m'ont emmené sur leur planète.*

Dr. Walter Seigmeister (1901–1965) created the field of Biosophy, the goals of which were to assure a nutritious diet for everyone, and the gradual elimination of the menstrual cycle. A longtime believer in hidden underground worlds, chance remarks made by polar explorer Richard Byrd led him to draw forth from his imagination the existence of an entire underground non-Dero civilization. *Flying Saucers from the Earth's Interior* (1960), written under his pseudonym Raymond Bernard, portrays the discs essentially as taxicabs, carrying messages and people to and from the world within; the title was later incorporated into his masterwork, *The Hollow Earth*. While searching fruitlessly for the entrance to the inner globe, he died of pneumonia in South America in 1965.

The following are reports told the writer in Brazil concerning Inner Earth people and flying saucers. There is no proof at all that these reports are true. They may be lies invented by the narrators in order to create an impression. But whether true or false they are interesting and show along what lines people are thinking today.

A Russian who formerly served in the Russian army said he and his troops once reached Lhasa, Tibet, where he was stationed some time, and there he came in touch with a secret society of Tibetan vegetarians who made regular trips by flying saucer through the North Polar opening to the hollow interior of the earth. He says he saw the saucer that made these trips. He said that the supreme object of all Tibetan lamas and yogis is to prepare their bodies to be worthy to be picked up by a flying saucer and carried to the hollow interior of the earth, whose human population consists mostly of Tibetan lamas and Oriental yogis, with very few Westerners, since Westerners are too bound to the things of this world, while lamas and yogis wish to escape from this miserable world and enter a much better world in the hollow interior of the earth.

The reason why subterranean people sent their flying saucers to us after the Hiroshima atomic explosion in 1945 was because they were afraid that further explosions might poison the air that comes into their interior atmosphere through the polar openings, coming from the outer air. Since inhabitants of other planets would have nothing to worry about if we poisoned our atmosphere by nuclear explosions, while inhabitants of the earth's interior, who receive their air from the outside atmosphere would have <u>plenty</u> to worry about, it is clear that flying saucers do not come from other planets but from the hollow interior of the earth.

— **Raymond Bernard, *Flying Saucers from the Earth's Interior*, p. 71**

Raymond Bernard. *Flying Saucers from the Earth's Interior: Evidence from Arctic Explorers Concerning the Existence of a Hollow Earth with Openings at the Poles into which Admiral Byrd, the Columbus who Discovered a New World, Penetrated for 2300, entering a Land of Mountains, Forests, Lakes, Rivers, Greenery and Animal Life - the Mysterious Land Beyond the Pole.* Santa Catarina, Brazil: R. Bernard, [ca, 1960s–70s]. Mimeographed pamphlet in wrappers, side stapled. 89 p. Illustrated.

In 1968 paranormal go-to paperback writer Brad Steiger (with the assistance of Joan Whritenour) turned out a one-shot magazine, *The Allende Letters* (1968), recounting in the most chill-a-minute way the tale of the mysterious experiment in Philadelphia, done in part due to the involvement of the Dero; the odd letters sent to Jessup, the unexplainable annotations in the copy of his book; mysterious men in black who may or may not have visited Jessup but certainly visited others, and the original Varo edition, copies of which supposedly brought death, or worse, to those who touched it (save, as noted, to Gray Barker).

Brad Steiger and Joan Whritenour. *The Allende Letters: Has the UFO Invasion Started?* New York: Universal Publishing and Distributing Corporation, 1968. Softcover pamphlet. Softcover, saddle stapled. 64 p. Illustrated. **Above:** Photo from p. 31.

Has the UFO invasion started?
THE ALLENDE LETTERS

A CHALLENGING NEW THEORY ON THE ORIGIN OF FLYING SAUCERS

By BRAD STEIGER and JOAN WHRITENOUR

EXCLUSIVE NEVER-BEFORE PUBLISHED UFO DOCUMENTS & PHOTOGRAPHS

The UFO Terrorists

The mysterious men in black are involved in a world-wide terrorist conspiracy to suppress the truth about flying saucers

We Want You

IS HITLER ALIVE ?

by
Michael X

Michael X [Barton]'s *We Want You: Is Hitler Alive?* (1960) was one of the first books to propose a South American/Nazi origin for the saucers, and as well suggest Hitler survived in one of the secret Argentine saucer bases. The elaborations on this theory have since been many.

Michael X. *We Want You!: [Is Hitler Alive?]*. Clarksburg, WV: Saucerian Books, 1969. Pamphlet in wrappers, saddle stapled. 39 p. Illustrated. Reprint, originally published: Los Angeles: Futura Press, 1960. Subtitle from cover.
Opposite: Illustration from Steiger and Whritenour, *The Allende Letters*, p. 15.

Paris Flammonde. *The Age of Flying Saucers: Notes on a projected history of unidentified flying objects.* New York, NY: Hawthorn Books, Inc., 1971. **Opposite top:** Photo and caption from jacket flap. **Opposite bottom:** Photo and caption from opposite p. 96.

Top: Paris Flammonde was for a number of years the producer of *The Long John Nebel Show*, which has acted as a "clearinghouse" for UFO reports and information. He is also the author of several other works, including the much acclaimed *The Kennedy Conspiracy*.

Bottom: Pauline Peavy is among the most intriguing of the subcultural personalities related to the Age of Flying Saucers. She is a medium who is in touch with "the Elders," the overspirits of the cosmos who rule all. (Sam Vandivert)

HANDS

THE TRUE ACCOUNT-
A HYPNOTIC SUBJECT
REPORTS ON OUTER SPACE

MARGARET WILLIAMS

LEE GLADDEN

Margaret Williams and Lee Gladden. *Hands: A True Case Study of a Phenomenal Hypnotic Subject.* Warner Springs, CA: Galaxy Press, 1976. Perfect bound in wrappers. xv, 272 p. Illustrated. **Following pages:** Illustration from p. 31.

Far and away the most peculiar and most obscure of all contactee narratives is *Hands* (1976), an account of how in 1957 a Beverly Hills psychiatrist and his weekly occult discussion group began one evening to channel a nameless, headless, eight-handed space alien whom they nicknamed "Hands" and who had much to say about very little.

"What is your name?'

"I have no name."

"No, I've just got hands."

"You've just got hands, but you're a person?"

"I'm a person with hands."

"You're a person with hands… are you a man or a woman?"

"Neither one." […]

"Are you one hand or two hands?"

"Neither."

"How many are you?"

"Eight."

"Eight hands!" I repeated. What kind of a monster had I here! … "What are your hands fastened to?" I asked.

"Their neck."

"What?"

"To their neck!"

"Uh, huh."

"Your neck?"

"'Of course.' — 'Who else's neck?' the entity must have thought."

— Margaret Williams and Lee Gladden, *Hands*, pp. 5–6

THE

FIRST

TELEPHOTO

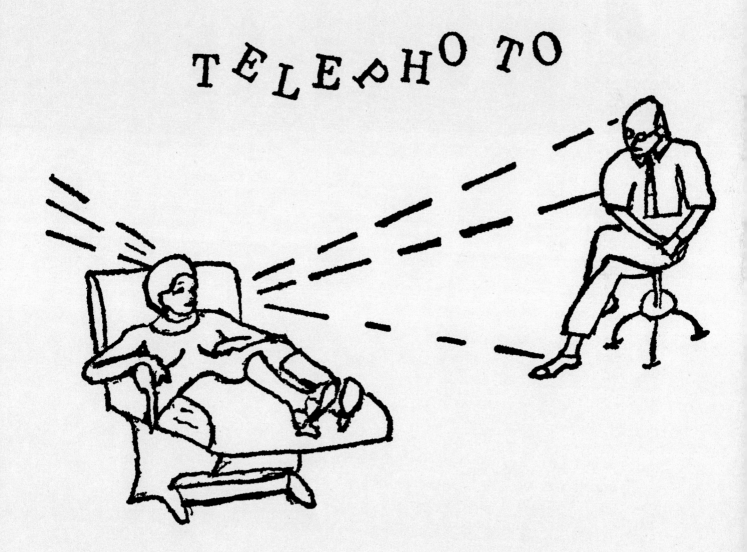

UFO
contact
from
UNDERSEA

2 December 1971, 15:00 Punta Norte, Peninsula de Valdez,
Province of Chubut, Argentina, facing Golfo San Matias.

Dr. Virgilio Sanchez-Ocejo
Lt. Col. Wendelle C. Stevens (Ret.)

UFO Contact from Undersea is yet another brick in the the Wendelle C. Stevens empire; this volume co-written with Virgilio Sanchez-Ocejo, provides a wealth of information on flying saucers, their comings and goings, their contacts with ocean life, all garnered via sessions of hypnotic regression discussing instances of earlier alien abductions.

Inside the ship there was a sound something like that of parrots, a great number of parrots. I could hear them perfectly but I could not see them. They must have had several cages for them installed in this ship. (Iris did not connect the parrot sounds to the beings at that time. As an afterthought one wonders if that might not have been the language of the beings themselves.)

**— Sanchez-Ocejo and Stevens,
UFO Contact from Undersea, p. 129**

Virgilio Sanchez-Ocejo and Wendelle C. Stevens. *UFO Contact from Undersea: A Report of the Investigation.* Tucson, AZ: Privately published by Wendelle C. Stevens, 1982. Imitation leatherbound with dust jacket. 190 p. Illustrated. Translated from Spanish original by Wendelle C. Stevens. **Opposite:** Illustration from p. 148.

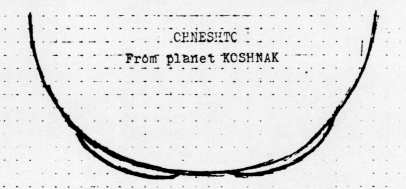

OHNESHTO
From planet KOSHNAK

Shallow turbin-like winding of light material around top of head.

A ten or twelve point star emblem seemed to be set in the cloth of the turbin. May have been some separate device mounted on the material.

The eyes were sloping wide almond-shaped bodies that came around the side of the head. No iris or pupil.

Whole eyeball was flecked with minute points of silvery light that seemed to scintillate.

Whole eyeball was the same "live looking" light green color.

Almost no earshell.

Two membrane covered pits in place of ear opening.

Nose was small and close to the face. Two nares entered the head more like our ear opening.

Jaw line was very stern looking and showed no emotion.

Mouth was small straight and thin lipped.

Chin was weak and rounded.

A drawing of an alien extraterrestrial being who called himself OHNESHTO and said that he came from a planet he called KOSHNAK in a star cloud in the star group we call Orion.

Cosmic End-Time
Secrets

Private Edition

by

Dr. Halsey

Dr. Wallace C. Halsey. *Cosmic End-Time Secrets.* Los Angeles: The Golden Dawn Press, 1965. Large Trade paperback, perfect bound with staples. 102 leaves. Illustrated. Private edition. **Opposite, top left and bottom:** Photos from p. 39, **top right:** photo from p. 4.

Tarna L. Halsey,
Dr. Halsey's lovely wife.

Tarna played the organ beautifully at Dr. Halsey's New-Age meetings although she never had a music lesson in her life. It is said that Tarna has almost total recall of a past lifetime on the mysterious planet Venus.

Dr. Wallace C. Halsey, D.D., L.L.D.

Noted UFO Researcher, electronic engineer, scholar of the scriptures, minister, author, founder of the Christ Brotherhood, Inc., and dedicated exponent of unlimited, Cosmic truth.

'FOR I WOULDST SPEAK TO THEE OF THE END-TIME, WHICH DRAWS NIGH — AND OF THE STRANGE AND WONDROUS THINGS I SHALL CAUSE TO BEFALL THEE...'

Dr. Wallace C. Halsey at his ranch. On the day this photo was taken the wind was blowing 20 to 30 knots per hour, yet this U.F.O. shaped cloud hovered above his ranch house for one hour. Photo is composite of two snapshots taken consecutively.

In *Night Siege: The Northern Ohio UFO-Creature Invasion* (1982) Dennis Pilichis takes a Keelian route, perceiving and then attempting to prove that mysterious paranormal agents drive both the UFO phenomenon as well as that of Bigfoot-like creatures. The title is an excellent example of the occasionally delirious crossover between ufology and cryptozoology.

> For lack of a better term, these "bigfoot critters" and the overlapping ufo
> activity exhibit a behavior which cannot now be explained or described
> in terms of known physical principles. There are paranormal occurances
> [sic] taking place, and they are functioning beyond what should occur if
> only the known laws of cause and effect are operating.

> — **Dennis Pilichis, *Night Siege*, p. 34**

Dennis Pilichis. *Night Siege: The Northern Ohio UFO-Creature Invasion.* Rome, OH: D. Pilichis. [1982]. Pamphlet in wrappers, saddle stapled. 39 p. Illustrated. **Opposite:** Illustration by L. Blazey from p. 28.

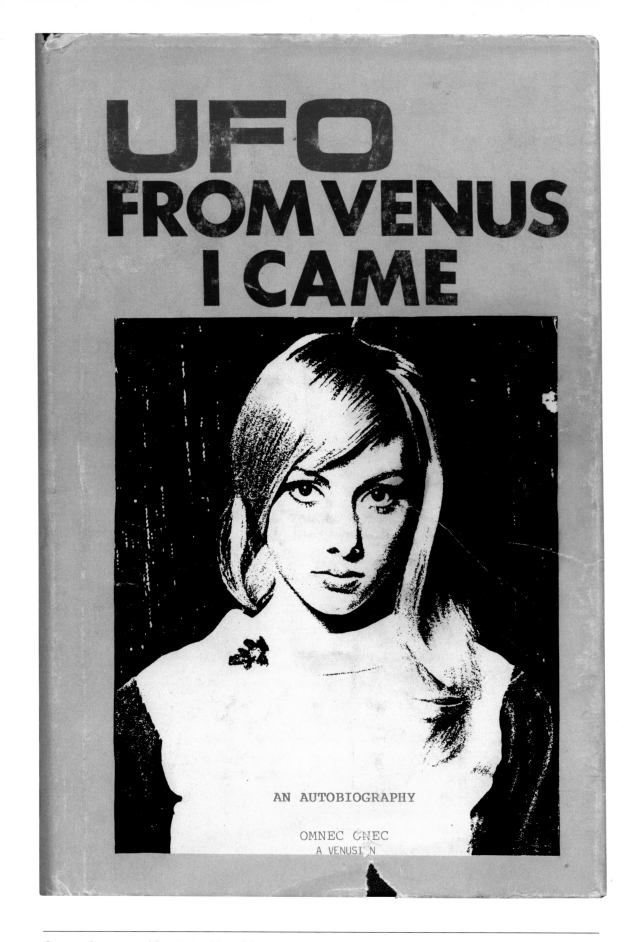

Omnec Onec, as told to Rainer Luedtke. *From Venus I Came.* Tucson, AZ: Privately published by W. C. Stevens, 1986. Imitation leatherbound with dust jacket. 280 p. Illustrated. Unnumbered copy from an edition of 1000. Cover title: *UFO: From Venus I Came.* **Following pages:** Illustration from p. 273.

Still readily reachable at www.omnec-onec.com, Omnec Onec writes in *UFO: From Venus I Came* that she was born nearly 250 Earth years ago in the Venusian city of Teutonia. When she first came to earth, she was substituted for a seven year-old girl who'd just died in a bus accident, and raised by the grandmother of "Sheila," the girl she'd replaced. After she reached adulthood, her Venusian persona returned to the fore, and she remembered she had come to earth to bring a message of peace and brotherhood.

A psychiatrist, I'm sure would have been called in to treat my overripe imagination and "save the poor child from a world of fantasy." Later in life the explanation would have sounded more sophisticated, if I would have made the mistake of talking. "There is no doubt that she is just a mixed-up kid from the backwoods of Tennessee. Her emotionally painful childhood sent her to seek escape in a dreamworld. Venus is a fantasyland in which to seek comfort, a place to find new meaning in life." Now that I have begun telling my story, I hear this reaction often. It does not offend me because I know it is due to a limited understanding.

— Omnec Onec and Rainer Luedtke, *From Venus I Came*, p. 37

Uncle Odin explained that larger vehicles called trucks were used to carry supplies to and from different cities. One city would have a factory while another may not, so the trucks were used to supply other cities with whatever was needed. People were paid with currency to drive the trucks.

Periodically, we made stops to eat, where I ate such things as hambergers and other foods very new to me. For dinner I ate a steak, and I liked that, but I did not care for the cooked vegetables because they were always overcooked. Green salads were delicious also.

I found that cow-meat was difficult to chew at first; some of it got stuck in my teeth, and we stopped to buy a tooth-brush. My uncle suggested that I keep my teeth very clean else they would decay.

He explained to me what restaurants were. People who did not care to cook for themselves or who were travelling would stop and have the food already prepared. In exchange, they had to part with a certain amount of currency.

— Omnec Onec and Rainer Luedtke, *From Venus I Came*, p. 192

Omnec's pencil sketch of the Temple City of Teutonia existing in the astral on Venus.

EXTRAORDINARY EVIDENCE

ELVIS
UFO
CONNECTION

Non-fiction Account
of Alien Intervention

THE LEGEND AND THE MYSTERY

by RICHARD DANIEL

Following the nationally reported experiences of Betty and Barney Hill in New Hampshire, abduction narratives took on an importance in the field about which the contactees could have only dreamed. By the 1980s the word "UFO" came to conjure in the popular mind not golden-haired space brothers and silver spacecraft, but rather gray-skinned midgets with slits for eyes, and a fondness for probes and sodomy. This last burst of renewed popular interest in the subject began to slacken and had pretty much pretty much faded out by the start of this century.

The Elvis-UFO Connection (1987), perhaps the most memorable of all such volumes on the subject, proposes that Elvis was long aware of his frequent excursions with alien beings, and that they helped him all along the way in his career, until they didn't. A jumpsuit accoutrement, a jeweled belt buckle bearing what are called herein "alien eyes," is proffered as evidence of interplanetary influence upon the King. It should come as no surprise that the author (Richard Daniel) is in fact two authors (Richard Vaculig and Daniel Guyll).

Richard Daniel. *The Elvis-UFO Connection: [Non-fiction Account of Alien Intervention: The Legend and the Mystery].* Woodinville, WA: Castle Rock Enterprises, 1987. Mass-market paperback. vi, 180 p. Subtitle from cover. **Opposite:** Illustration from title page.

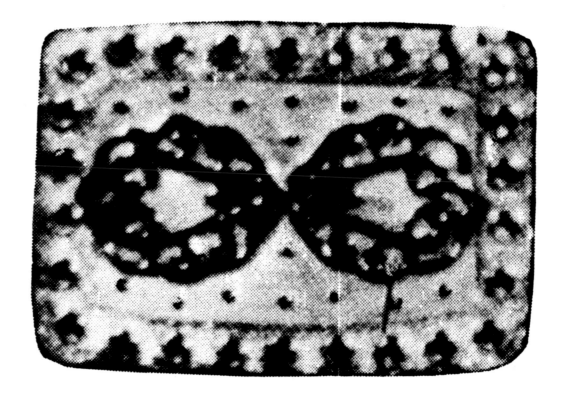

For the next nine years, Elvis is left to do his magic and at age twenty-nine, the visitors re-enter the scene. Elvis is to receive a thought impulse designed to tie the urgings of his brother's voice to ideals which will assist him in reaching higher awareness: 'do good, live a good life and lead others'. Elvis' compulsion to study matters of the spirit is meant to be a struggle, for it is only through conflict and friction that the rough edges of a stone are made smooth.

The following thirteen years become increasingly confusing for Elvis. In his mind is the awareness of the existence of the visitors, accompanied by his compulsion to search for the meaning of it all but something tells him time is running out. In the end, time ceases to exist for Elvis' physical being. The body of his soul is channeled into another dimension where it waits to be recycled in the year prophesied to be one of great cleansing—2001.

No one knows for sure if and how this will take place. What seems apparent at this time is that the ultimate purpose for Elvis' physical existence was to have him attract masses of humanity. The gift he was given to accomplish that objective was his voice.

— **Richard Daniel**, *The Elvis-UFO Connection*, pp. 133–134

Gabriel Green (1924–2001), one of the last old school contactees, founded the Amalgamated Flying Saucer Clubs of America Inc. in 1957. Not long earlier he'd met saucer crewmen from the planet Korender, which orbits Alpha Centauri, and maintained regular telepathic correspondence afterward, generally regarding the imminent return of Jesus in a flying saucer. Green's one book, *Let's Face the Facts About Flying Saucers* (1967) is a farrago of brief saucer accounts with no direct Korendian connection. He ran for President as a write-in candidate in 1960 and 1972. He didn't win.

Norton Novitt, an amateur scientist from Denver, Colorado, whose hobby is the study of the electric properties of insects, believes it is highly likely that Unidentified Flying Objects are nothing more than glowing swarms of luminous flying ants.

— **Gabriel Green,** *Let's Face the Facts About Flying Saucers,* **p. 77**

What "message" have the spacemen given contactees?

They are here to impart part of their advanced scientific, technological, and sociological knowledge to help us resolve the problems of mankind before we destroy ourselves. The contactees say spacemen were attracted by our nuclear explosions and they're concerned that mankind may destroy itself and part of the universe.

They hope to enlighten us to successfully eliminate the motives for war, expansionism, and poverty. Several of the contactees have pointed out that the extraterrestrials use an advanced system of economics that has eliminated want and need on their planets.

— **Gabriel Green,** *Let's Face the Facts About Flying Saucers,* **p. 125**

How can I learn more about saucers?

Maintain an open mind, read some of the better books on the subject, and keep informed on current developments. If you wish, you can write AFSCA and obtain my list of recommended books.

— **Gabriel Green,** *Let's Face the Facts About Flying Saucers,* **p. 127**

Gabriel Green, with Warren Smith. *Let's Face the Facts About Flying Saucers.* New York: Popular Library, 1967. Mass-market paperback. 127 p.

GABRIEL GREEN

President, Amalgamated Flying Saucer Clubs of America

LET'S FACE THE FACTS ABOUT FLYING SAUCERS

FOR THE FIRST TIME ANYWHERE—EXCLUSIVE—
UNCENSORED: THE TRUTH ABOUT UNIDENTIFIED
FLYING OBJECTS—BY THE ONLY MAN WHO KNOWS
THE U.F.O. STORY *FROM THE INSIDE* ● ● ● ● ● ● ●

CETO'S NEW FRIENDS

Leah A. Haley

Illustrated by Lisa Dusenberry

Leah Haley's *Ceto's New Friends* (1993) tells children it'll be OK if aliens come to take them from their houses into space–they won't hurt you. Somewhere, the Dero emit evil chuckles.

Leah A. Haley; illustrated by Lisa Dusenberry. *Ceto's New Friends.* Tuscaloosa, AL: Greenleaf Publications, 1994. In paper-covered boards. [32] p. Illustrated. **Opposite:** Illustrations by Dusenberry from pp. 7, 17, 18, & 23.

Ceto cannot talk with his mouth. He talks with his eyes.

He taught them how to talk with their eyes.

He let them punch bright colored buttons.

The white light took them down from the spaceship.

Virgil T. Godwin

Other stories by this author...

Virginia City Joker
This is a comstock story of the early eighteen hundreds, based on true facts.

Second World of 2403
Based on a realistic plot.

Big Red
The first female construction company in Oregon

Commander X. *Underground Alien Bases.* [New Brunswick, N.J.?]: Abelard Productions, Inc., 1990. Trade paperback, perfect bound. 127 p. Illustrated. Special limited edition. **Opposite:** Illustration from p. 87. "Researcher John J. Robinson talked to one individual who said he saw this being standing guard near a cave entrance." **Virgil T. Godwin.** *The Bizarre Shaver.* [N.p.: Privately published], 1980. Trade paperback, perfect bound. 163 p. **Above:** Back cover.

Christa Tilton of Tulsa, Oklahoma experienced a terrifying abduction at the hands of aliens who took her to their underground base in Dulce, New Mexico.

Commander X. *Underground Alien Bases.* **Above:** Photo from p. 41. **Opposite:** Illustration from p. 51.

Boulders

David Huggins, New Jersey. Adult male. Huggins painted in 1987 based on physical, daytime encounter in 1950s at his central Georgia farm home. 'These Little Guys seemed to float down out of the sky. They seemed to be able to appear and disappear.'

Linda Moulton Howe. *Glimpses of Other Realities. Volume I: Facts and Eyewitnesses.* Huntingdon Valley, Penn.: LMH Productions, 1993. Trade paperback, perfect bound. xxii, 365 p. Illustrated. First edition, first printing, Dec, 1993. Illustration by David Huggins from p. 263.

Gray being wearing high-collared cape seen repeatedly in the many abduction esperiences of adult female Jeanne Robinson since she was four years old. Drawn by Jeanne Robinson in Springfield, Missouri.

L.P. Bakerfield, California. Adult female. Drawn in 1990 based on teenage experience.

On the afternoon of [October] 11th, [1973] 19-year-old Calvin Parker [left] and 42-year-old Charles Hickson [right] were fishing at the mouth of the Pascagoula River. Becoming aware of a buzzing sound, the two men—both workers in a nearby shipyard—looked behind them and saw a large, glowing oval-shaped object. [...] Petrified with fear at this sight, the two watched as a door appeared out of nowhere in the object and three strange beings moved toward them. Instead of walking, they seemed to float and didn't move their legs. In appearance, they were about five feet in height, had bullet-like heads with no necks, slits for mouths, and, where their ears and noses would be, had thin cone-shaped appendages that stuck straight outward. The percipients said the beings had no eyes, had round feet and clawed hands, and wrinkled grayish skin. (Opposite, a sketch of one of the occupants made by the workers' superintendent.)

Two of the humanoids seized Hickson; the third grabbed Parker who, overcome with fright, passed out. Hickson claimed he was "floated" aboard the UFO and presently found himself in a brightly lit room. As the two ufonauts held him, an eye-like device appeared in mid-air and Hickson's body was moved about in front of it in what he took to be an examination. When this was over, he was simply left hanging in mid-air and he could not move a muscle. Some 20 minutes from the time he first saw the UFO, Hickson was floated out of it and put on the ground. With Parker weeping and praying near him, he watched the UFO rise straight up and fly out of sight.

— **David C. Knight,** *UFOs: A Pictorial History from Antiquity to the Present*, **p. 179**

David C. Knight. *UFOs: A Pictorial History from Antiquity to the Present*. New York: McGraw-Hill Book Company, 1979. **Above and opposite:** Photos and illustration from p. 178.

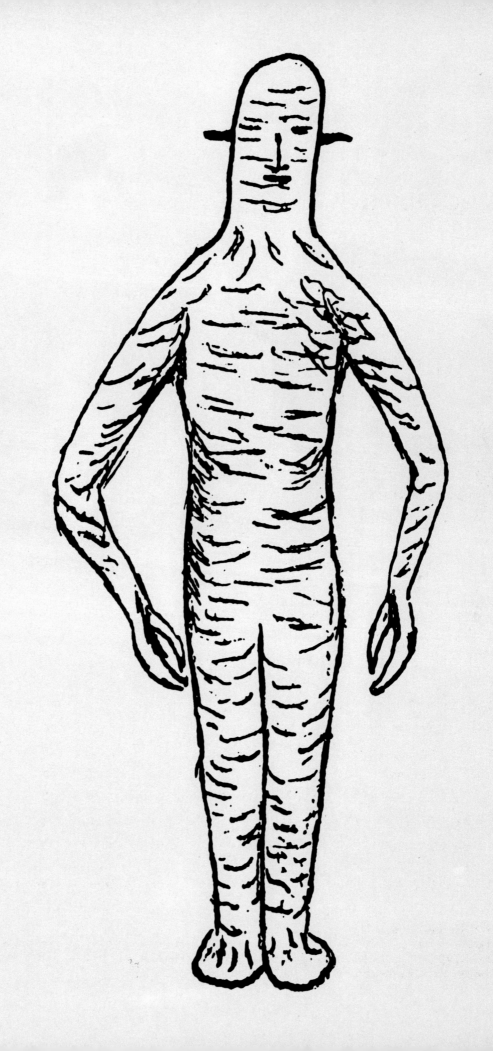

 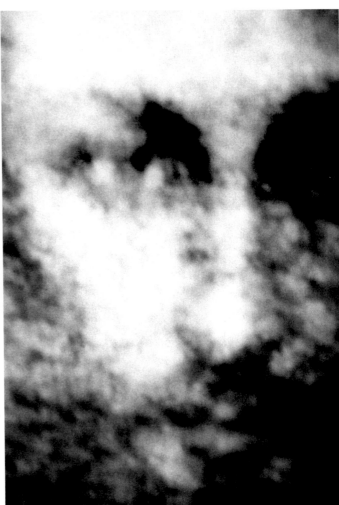

Top left: Author George C. Andrews with the Crystal Skull (Bryan Myers). **Top right:** Maurizio Cavallo, an abductee who has had contact with the Blonds, took this photograph immediately following the departure of the aliens. He was suddenly moved to photograph a section of a blank wall in his studio. When the film was developed, this image appeared on the frame that seemed to have been wasted on a section of plain blank wall. (Maurizio Cavallo, Centro Ricerche Clarion, C.P. 45, 13100 Vercelli, Italy) **Opposite:** Jeff and Steve Lowe, from Beavercreek Township, Ohio, proved that a 200-foot roll of aluminum foil can make two Martians.

George C. Andrews. *Extra-terrestrial Friends and Foes.* Lilburn, Ga.: IllumiNet Press, 1993. Trade paperback, perfect bound. 359 p. Illustrated. **Above:** Photos from pp. 103 and 104. **Morris Goran.** *The Modern Myth: Ancient Astronauts and UFOs.* South Brunswick and New York/London: A.S. Barnes and Company/Thomas Yoseloff Ltd, 1978. Hardcover book, clothbound with dust jacket, 192 p. Illustrated. **Opposite:** Photo from p. 120.

When James Templeton took this picture of his daughter Elizabeth on a family outing near Carlisle, England, in May 1964, no one saw the figure in a 'spacesuit' behind her.

Bob Teets. *West Virginia UFOs: Close Encounters in the Mountain State.* Terra Alta, W.V.: Headline Books, 1995. Trade paperback, perfect bound. x, 213 p. Illustrated. **Opposite:** Illustration from p. 121. **Jerome Clark.** *The UFO Encyclopedia, Volume 3: High Strangeness: UFOs from 1960 Through 1979.* Detroit, MI: Omnigraphics, Inc., 1996. Hardcover book in glossy paperboard boards, no jacket. xxvi, 777 p. Illustrated. **Above:** Photo from p. 474.

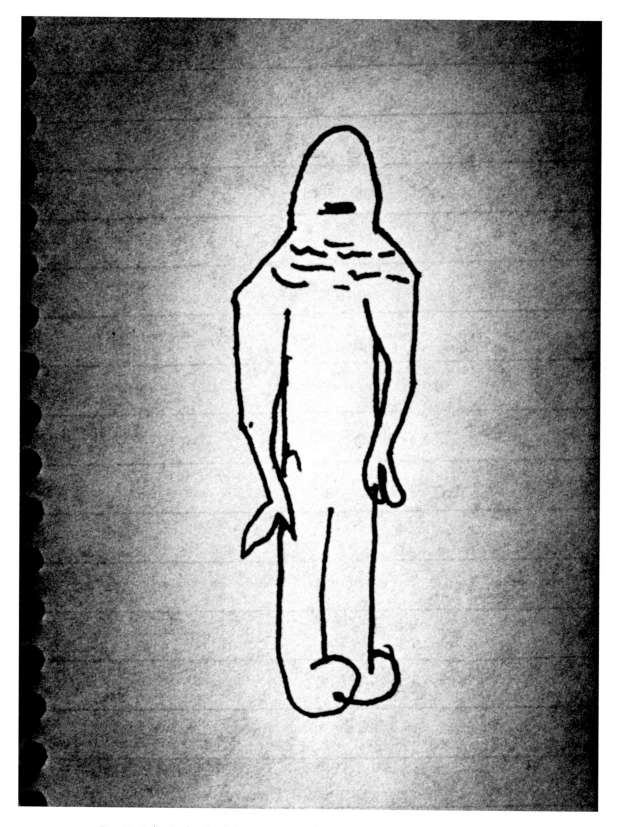

Fig. 8: Calvin's sketch of the creature made in April, 1975. He admits the facial details were not clear to him because his vision was becoming blurred. Upon entering the ship Calvin lost consciousness.

Fig. 23: Charlie took me squirrel hunting on the tree farm where he claims he had his first post-abduction "contact" experience. Here he sits as he did that January afternoon when he witnessed the return of the alien craft and received a reassuring telepathic message. This is only the beginning of the "repeater" problem.

Charles Hickson and William Mendez. *UFO Contact at Pascagoula.* Tucson, Ariz.: Wendelle C. Stevens, 1983. Hardcover book, clothbound with dust jacket. 274 p. Illustrated. **Opposite:** Photo from p. 60. **Above:** Photo from p. 178.

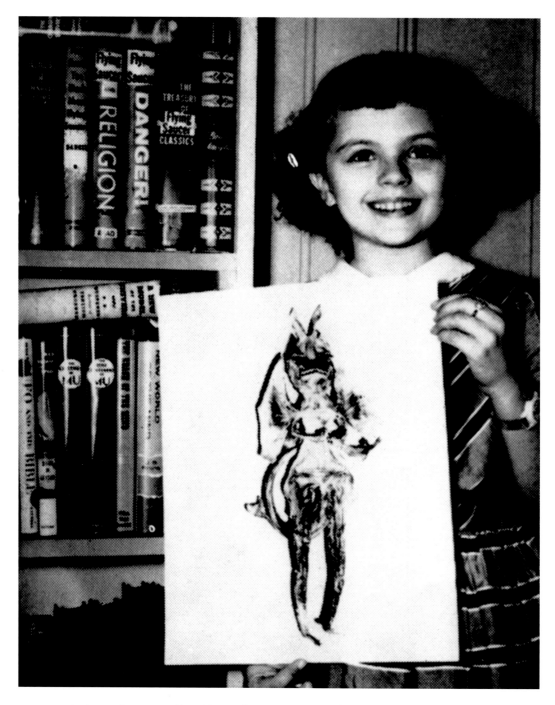

Is this a distant neighbor? (See Chapter Six, example A) Judith Ann Conroy, the photographer's niece, holds a sketch of a supposed 'little man from space'.

Frank E. Stranges. *Flying Saucerama.* New York: Vantage Press, 1959. Clothbound, 115 p. + [24] p. of plates. Illustrated. **Above:** Photo from p. 39.

Mrs. May, holding a drawing of the Flatwoods entity made for the 'We the People'
TV show, 1952. Photo taken by Gray Barker.

William L. Moore. *The Flatwoods Monster Revisited: New Revelations About One of the Most Famous UFO Cases of the 1950s.* Burbank, Calif.: The Fair-Witness Project, 1993. Photocopied softcover, side stapled. [12] leaves. Illustrated. "[Publication] #1307." **Above:** Illustration from p. 11.

See....FLYING SA